THE TROUBLE
WITH GABRIELLE

Sylvia Hubbard

HubBooks Literary - Detroit

The Trouble With Gabrielle © 2021 Sylvia Hubbard

All rights reserved.
ISBN: 9798494314871
Check out more of this author's book at
http://sylviahubbard.com/books

This is a work of fiction. Names, characters, places, and incidents either are the product of the author's imagination or are used fictitiously, and any resemblance to actual person, living or dead, business establishments, events, or locales, is entirely coincidental.
This book, or parts thereof, may not be reproduced in any form without permission.

License Notes

This book is licensed for your personal enjoyment only. This book may not be re-sold or given away to other people. If you would like to share this book with another person, please purchase an additional copy for each recipient. If you're reading this book and did not purchase it, or it was not purchased for your use only, then please return to author's website and purchase your own copy. Thank you for respecting the hard work of this author.

DISCLAIMER: This story is intended for a mature audience only! Contains explicit, graphic sex and language, include rough and aggressive sex, dirty talk and more. Not intended for individuals under the age of 18 or those with a weak constitution.

For information address:
Sylvia Hubbard | Visit her website at:
http://SylviaHubbard.com

Book Website
http://sylviahubbard.com/troublewithgabrielle

Contents

PROLOGUE 1
CHAPTER 1 Ten Years Later 9
CHAPTER 2 Three months later 13
CHAPTER 3 You're Who?! You're What?! 21
CHAPTER 4 Should She Stay or Should She Go? 27
CHAPTER 5 The day she met him! 35
CHAPTER 6 Oliver Was Right! 43
CHAPTER 7 Can He Touch You? 49
CHAPTER 8 Who Murdered Nancy? 55
CHAPTER 9 Not your average ten-year-old 65
CHAPTER 10 Possibly Blowing this out of proportion 73
CHAPTER 11 May I Touch You 83
CHAPTER 12 I know what the problem is 91
CHAPTER 13 Taking full advantage in his weakness 97
CHAPTER 14 Beautiful but deadly 105
CHAPTER 15 You owe me no explanation 111
CHAPTER 16 It was abnormal, but she liked it. 119
CHAPTER 17 I should go 125
CHAPTER 18 Too much sleep 131
CHAPTER 19 Oh where did my little boy go 139
CHAPTER 20 Let him Drink 145
CHAPTER 21 What's wrong with you? 151
CHAPTER 22 There's something wrong with him 157
CHAPTER 23 You're life is my life 163
CHAPTER 24 Give Solace 169
CHAPTER 25 This can't be happening again 177
CHAPTER 26 You Should Have Died! 183

CHAPTER 27 He Knew All Along..193
CHAPTER 28 She's gone..199
ABOUT THIS AUTHOR:..207

PROLOGUE

"This will be for the best," her mother had said, but only because she didn't want Gabrielle to live in her home and mess up the situation with the new boyfriend.

Ingrid Payne had more boyfriends than Ford had made cars, but this was "extra special." This meant he paid the bills and put up with Ingrid in her drunken rage.

Gabrielle held her cheek, remembering the many times her mother had slapped her across the room, highly intoxicated and just angry about nothing.

When Gabrielle was young, she lived away from her mother until she was seventeen. If she didn't camp out on a friend's couch, then she was sleeping on the streets somewhere in Detroit. Either way, Gabrielle had always taken care of herself and didn't ask for much.

She returned to Ingrid because, to go to college, she needed an address. She gave Ingrid every penny she earned, but that still wasn't enough to appease the woman. Ingrid wanted more money.

When a friend begged Gabrielle to "take a job" as an escort, Gabrielle needed the money to stay in school and have somewhere to live. She was told the guy was handsy but never wanted sex. Gabrielle didn't mind doing the job. She'd done others for a couple of Jacksons without hesitation. Most were older men that liked to touch and took too much medication to be sustainable. Accepting money and looking like their dime piece for a nice dinner was nothing, while later on, letting them drool over her while she jerked them off didn't faze her moral compass.

She did what she had to do, and this job tonight was supposed to be no different.

Yet, it had not been.

Gabrielle remembered every moment of that night. The moment she had entered the elevator to go up to the hotel room, she felt different. As she waited for the doors to open, she checked her wristband with extra money, a condom, and several mouth guards just in case. There was also a tiny pick for her safety. On her other wristband was a refillable bottle of lube she could easily squirt out and use for her line of work.

All of this wrapped securely around her wrist, matching the dark blue after five flowing, knee-length maxi and dark blue three-inch heels to lift her thick calves to accentuate the curvy all-natural coke bottle figure.

On a warm September night, she went up into the five-star hotel room to spend no less than two hours there and then leave.

Checking the mirror in the elevator, she quickly surveyed the light makeup she had put on. With her light almond skin, contrasting with her kinky black nape length twist out, she felt comfortable enough in her size fourteen, thick thighs body with a tiny waist to carry the outfit she was wearing.

This client had specified company and dinner; Like the other ones, "company" meant good talk before giving a hand job. These medium-income white guys just wanted the idea of being around a black woman. They never wanted to go all the way, and she could make a good two hundred a night giving them excellent talk and touch.

He opened the door, and she was struck at how devilishly handsome he was. The drugs and alcohol had done a number on his appearance through years of abuse, yet the foundational gorgeousness could not be ignored.

Too bad. Suppose he had stayed away from taking too many substances: In that case, he might've been a very irresistible five-foot eleven Arabic man with a swagger that reminded her of the actor Dev Patel, but this stranger was a little thicker in build, clean-shaven, and broad shouldered.

"Oliver Farnsworth," he introduced with a smile extending his hand like a gentleman.

That was not an Arabic name, and his voice had no accent, which meant he was either born in America and educated or had figured out how to drop his accent altogether.

"Gabrielle Payne," she returned, caught off guard because she never gave her real name before, yet he had these grayish-brown eyes on an Arab man she hadn't expected. Murky and naughty, like she was looking into the soul of Loki.

"You're cute," he said, moving out of the doorway and letting her in.

"You aren't so bad yourself," she lightly teased back to hide her nervousness as she entered the posh hotel room.

Oliver smiled again. "Ole girl, you do know how to brighten a man's night when he's not feeling like being brightened." He gave her body an entire visual inspection. "You're different. Not what I expected. Fresh."

Listening to the door close behind her, she forced herself to relax and take in her surroundings.

Noting the personal items around, she concluded he had been living there a while, and he seemed to have sequestered himself inside - not leaving out hardly. Old room service trays were on tables, and the coffee station had other snacks around other than what the hotel provided. Gabrielle could usually tell a lot about someone by their personal space.

"Isn't that why you called on me?" She went over to the bar and looked at the liquor he'd already been drinking. "What is your flavor?"

"Anything that will make me drunk and forget this life," he said and sighed longingly as if wishing death would be the next to knock on the door.

Gabrielle steeled herself not to react to his depressing remark. Most likely, it could be the alcohol talking.

She saw the janitor's coveralls thrown over a chair and frowned. It was strange for a man living in a nice hotel to see a work uniform with his name on the chest.

Getting him comfortable, she asked, "How old are you, Oliver?"

"Thirty-five," he said proudly. "And you? Oh wait, let me guess."

She finished pouring his drink and waited for his guess knowing already it would be wrong.

"Twenty-two?" he attempted.

Frowning, she said, "Twenty-eight," she corrected.

He was surprised. "You look so young."

"Black don't crack," she sang as she started over to the couch again. Her youthful appearance always threw people off, and most thought she was too young and innocent to be in the game. Most times, she never corrected anyone about how old she was and allowed them to believe whatever they wanted to think.

Tonight, was different. This man made her feel differently. "Oliver, tell me what troubles you," she urged and prepared for the earful.

"Life," he said, and for a long moment, he didn't speak. Staring pensively at his drink, he said, "As I was getting off work, I got a call from my father's lawyer. I thought it was to tell me I'd pissed him off enough to cut me off like he'd done my brother." He moved his hand over her thigh. "But then I remembered I'd never slept with a black woman."

She raised a brow. "I don't think you've paid for those services tonight, and you ordered the wrong woman." Changing the subject, she said, "Your father's lawyer wanted something important?"

"Good avoidance, Gabrielle," He said with a chuckle. "He let me know my father died."

"I'm sorry," she said, grievous.

"Don't be. He wasn't a very nice man. He disowned his oldest son from his birthright and forced the family to turn away from him in his time of need."

Gasping, Gabrielle said, "Was this a good thing for you?"

"For years, I felt guilty knowing I was going to take my brother's birthright away. David has been sick all his life. He had nothing going for him except the business. I walked away from everything. I still feel guilty, and I've always wanted to do something," He gave her a long visual perusal again.

She felt like a smoky hot dog to his bun, and he was trying to see how to get her to fit. "But now that your father is dead, can your brother take over the company now?"

"No, my father made it very difficult for David to walk in and take it, but that isn't my real problem." He finished his drink and stared hard into the empty glass as if the weight of the world was on his shoulders. "I have seventy-two hours to return to my family's home and take over the family business, or I lose everything to my stepmother, who by the way would do anything to be a grandmother. I literally won't have kids just because it would make her happy. And I'm too damn vindictive to allow that woman to have my brother's birthright."

Gabrielle went to get him another drink, unsure if he was telling her his miserable life to make her feel comfortable or telling her this to get it off his chest.

Either way, she listened as he removed his jacket and then his tie.

Joining him on the couch again, as she handed him a drink, she asked, "Where do you work?" Gabrielle placed the extra napkins she had swiped from the bar on the table in front of them, knowing she would need them later.

He looked away, ashamed. "I'm working for a competing delivery company." Pressing his fingers to his lips, he said, "Shhh... they don't know who I am." Chuckling more to himself, he admitted, "My brother would have a field day making fun of me about that. He never thought I'd do a lick of hard work in my life." Oliver nodded to the uniform. "I'm stupid to stay here, but I can't imagine staying anywhere else." He fondly rubbed the couch.

"Why would your brother think you'd never work hard in your life?" she asked to keep him talking.

Oliver swigged the drink she had handed him and then chuckled miserably, "I'm not a very good person."

To admit that out loud to someone else seemed strange, but Oliver said it with such ease that she had to believe him.

Yet, Gabrielle had not felt he was a faulty person, and she only took people at face value or how they treated her.

Putting her emotions on hold, she knew that she couldn't get close to her clients in her line of work, but Oliver had this pull. She needed to get down to business before she found herself enamored by this man. "You're not a bad person, Oliver?" she said and reached over to open his pants.

He relaxed enough for her to reach into his pants and remove a very prominent member. Scooting closer, Gabrielle took her time, using his breathing as an indication of his needs. When he held his breath, she knew he liked what she did, and when he breathed deeply, he needed the long strokes. Every once in a while, she would rub her finger over the tip heightening his pleasure and loving how his body would tweak in enjoyment.

"Wait..." he begged breathlessly, moving his hand down and halting her.

Reaching in his jacket, he pulled out his wallet and tossed five one-hundred-dollar bills on the small table in front of them.

"You can have that only if you're naked when you finish jacking me off," he offered.

"Why?" she questioned.

"Because I've never seen a black woman naked. All my life, I've been groomed not to be attracted to black women. I figure since I'm crossing the line, I might as well go all the way."

She needed the money, but she usually would draw the line at nakedness.

Still, he was cute, and he seemed to need brightening up. If looking upon her body would cheer him up, maybe this one good deed could help her get into heaven.

Standing up, Gabrielle took her time taking her clothes off, keeping eye contact with those beautiful gray-brown eyes. They were almost a tannish-brown and mesmerizing to stare into as they seemed to caress every part of her body while she revealed to him pieces of her she had not shown to a man in a long time. She removed everything except her wristbands and shoes.

"You're beautiful," he said in a whisper.

"Thank you," she said.

"No, I don't think you know how beautiful you are. May I?" he asked, scooting to the end of the couch.

He was fully dressed, and Gabrielle felt at ease, so she nodded.

His hands were strong as they pressed on the side of her waist and then moved down her thighs. "Your skin is like the caramel my grandmother would make from scratch. I remember she watched the pot as she mixed in the ingredients and told me caramel only has one good color to be perfect. You are that color." By this time, his hands were moving up the front of her thighs, past her womanhood, and then over her stomach.

Butterflies were zooming under her stomach, feeling like they were about to burst forth from her belly button.

Get it together, Gabrielle, she told herself. Oddly, she wanted to be professional about this and not succumb to lustful intentions.

Taking control of her situation, she knelt in front of him and gently pushed his body back with one hand and wrapped her hands around the base of his manhood with the other. Her hands were well lubed, so he immediately gave in to her strokes. She knew her hands could jack a man off in her sleep, and she didn't need to give him any special attention, but she wanted to give him what he had given her.

Something nice and different.

She gave him her utmost attention, extracting every tiny bit of pleasure until he was clutching the couch, and his hips bolted up at the exact moment he hit his peak. At the same time, she pressed her finger on his perineum to hold back the powerful orgasm, and the sob of anguish shot out of his lips.

"What the hell, woman?!" he retched in distress.

"Shhh..." she teased and sent him reeling as she softly blew at the tip, but at the same time continued to massage the base of him. "Deep breaths," she ordered.

He was immediately back to the peak, his head reeling back and his eyes rolled back in his head.

"In through your nose and out through your mouth," she whispered instructions. "Let me make you happy, Oliver."

He sobbed, and tears rolled down his cheek as he trembled. Following her instructions, Oliver took large gulps of air and then blew them out.

Gabrielle took his body from the edge and then back again until he was almost out of his mind.

It wasn't until he was begging for release, did she allow him.

And Oliver cried in gratitude.

She allowed him to gather himself as she used the napkins to clean him up and then herself. When she started to reach for her dress, he stopped her.

7

"Wait," he said, still breathing hard. "Can I lay with you?"

Everything inside of her told her to say no, but looking up into his eyes, she saw a man filled with so much pain and heartache.

Cupping his face, she asked, "Who hurt you?"

"Everyone," he said in a wounded breath.

Without denying him, she nodded and climbed on the couch with him. He stayed fully clothed, but she noted he didn't close his pants. Yet, she didn't make a big deal about him. A man his age and deterioration would most likely not recover for about thirty minutes.

They laid there quietly for a long moment. Oliver's arm moved around her waist, and when she looked down at his wrist, she noted there were a lot of healed slits on his arm. He'd attempted to kill himself.

"Why do you do this?" he questioned.

Shrugging, she said her usual statement when asked this question. "A woman's gotta do what she has to do to survive."

"Someone didn't love you?"

"Maybe I don't deserve love," she said.

"You're not a bad person, Gabrielle." His lips were close to her ear. "I know bad people, and you're far from what they are, no matter what you do. Deep down, you're just trying to make something good out of a bad situation."

Keeping her soul out of her profession was difficult when the deep soothing cull of his voice and the nakedness of her body being heated by his warmth opened her spirit.

"Can I ask you to stay until it's over?"

"Over? For what?" she questioned.

"Just stay, Gabrielle. Just stay with me."

Maybe it's because he said her real name, or perhaps because the truth was more brutal to hear in her vulnerable state. Quite possibly, it could be both.

Laying in his arms, Gabrielle felt her entire world collide. All her emotions seem to pull together and pour from her. "Yes, I can stay. I will stay with you, Oliver."

Chapter 1

Ten Years Later

One dark and stormy night, a knock on the door and Oliver appeared.

"I need to talk some more," he said, smelling heavily of alcohol.

The feeling of seeing him brought back memories of the last night they were together ten years ago, and Gabrielle could feel her body aching. Dammit, how could her attraction to him lay dormant for a decade? "I take it you've decided not to take your medication and decided the bottom of a bottle was so much better?" her tone of voice was filled with sarcasm.

Oliver snorted. "I hate medicine, ole girl. Damn depressants get in the way of the alcohol's effects. I love drinking too much, Gabrielle. Please let me in."

Charles was asleep so letting Oliver inside her apartment was no problem. He was still worse for wear but clean-shaven and in a much more expensive suit than last time she had initially seen him. Plus, he called her a familiar endearment from their first night. Gabrielle couldn't resist. "Rough night?" she questioned, leaning against the door.

He looked deep into her eyes and countered, "How the hell have you not aged a day, Gabrielle?"

She smiled because most people didn't call her by her full name. At work, everyone just called her Gabby or Gabs. "Thank you, but I can't say the same for you, Oliver." She wasn't curious as to how he found her. Oliver had found her bank account on his own ten years ago and started making payments to her without asking whether she was pregnant or not from the three days they had spent together.

Those payments allowed her to quit the escort business, get her education and be the woman she was today.

Indicating he could enter, Gabrielle moved out of the way. "I don't have any alcohol for you, Oliver," she said.

"That's fine," he said, taking out a silver flask with his initials engraved and offered her some after he took a swig. "I brought my own."

She shook her head. "I think I'm going to need all my wits about me tonight and especially tomorrow. Charles is taking his college entrance exam."

"Seriously?" He looked down at his expensive watch. "It's been that long?"

Gabrielle laughed and covered her mouth so she wouldn't wake up her son sleeping right above their heads. "No, silly. He's only going to be ten soon, but he's excelled in his studies so fast his teachers made him eligible to start taking college classes."

"He's like my brother," Oliver said proudly. "David's a smart-ass bastard. It was difficult to keep up with him."

"Well, Charles certainly has his father's penchant for slacking, don't worry. I can't get him to do a chore unless he wants a new game." She guided him to the back family room and closed the door for privacy.

"At least I can do something my horrible brother can't do," Oliver said proudly. "Bastard has kidney disease. He's impotent and too damn proud to ask for my kidney."

"Why don't you give it to him, Oliver?" she asked exasperated.

Oliver smiled mischievously. "I like to see him squirm because I know he would never ask. Pride before the storm when it comes to David." He took another swig of the flask.

"You never made me ask for anything, Oliver," she pointed out, taking the flask away and setting it across the room.

"Because you're Gabrielle. You're magic."

She didn't know if he was drunk or serious. "You shouldn't make your brother ask for something he needs, Oliver," she reprimanded. "You should give it to him. He's your brother."

"You talk like a mother, and you'd think differently if you met David. Plus, you're an only child. Seeing your siblings squirm is so much fun."

"Okay," Gabrielle negotiated. "Make David squirm a little more and then offer it. What harm can it do? You're not doing much with it."

Oliver walloped in laughter.

Turning on some soft music to camouflage their voices, she joined him on the couch where he'd already gotten comfortable.

This was supposed to be another bedroom, but she had made it into a small family room to keep the television and computer out of her son's bedroom. Otherwise, Charles would never sleep.

"You're probably right, plus, there are other things I have accomplished David doesn't have," he said proudly.

"Like?" she asked since he was so generously talking about his brother. Last time he hadn't been so loose lipped about his brother, so he must be drunker than last time.

"David can't be in control of the company. He pissed my father off when we were young by dating some black girl. Told my father exactly where he could put his share of the company, and my father did so."

She gasped. "But you did the same thing."

"No," he denied, winking wickedly. "I never dated you. And no one knows about you."

Her feelings were not hurt as he pointed this out. "Is David still married?"

Oliver shook his head. "His wife died five years ago of cancer. It took ten long fucking years for her to die, and then his ass disappeared across the ocean. Son of a bitch."

She covered Oliver's mouth because he was getting louder. As she shot him a warning with her eyes, he kissed her palm.

"We're not going to be mean here, Oliver," she insisted.

He nodded and fondly pushed a cowlick from her face. She'd pressed out her hair recently for Charles' recent graduation from his pre-collegiate programs. Keeping it natural saved so much money, and she never knew how to style her hair when it was pressed out, so wearing two-strand twists always worked for her eighteen inches of 4c hair.

"You still have the most beautiful skin color, Gabrielle," he said and kissed her cheek. "David used to be enchanted by the caramel color too. Can I taste you?"

"You still are charming as shit, Oliver," she said, loving how she enjoyed how good he looked. She'd met and dated other men, but Oliver's gorgeousness was just too delicious. Unfortunately, his penchant for drinking, depression, and other characteristics made it difficult to be fully attracted to him. As a mother, she knew Oliver would not make a good role model for her son, even though this was his father.

"I'm a son of a bitch," he said. "I know, and for the strangest reason, you still like me."

"Like is a little strong," she countered in a tease.

Oliver leaned in close to her until their noses touched. "I'm going to make love to you tonight, Gabrielle. I need to."

She remembered that tone so long ago and knew she could not resist him. On top of that, she'd kept celibate for so long; the man could've just told her he'd come for a booty call, and she'd agreed to anything.

"Good," she admitted. "Cause I need some love-making."

He chuckled. "Want to go to your room?"

"No, we'll wake up Charles, but this couch turns into a bed."

Oliver had her permission. They'd talk later, and she probably wouldn't get much sleep, but that was fine.

He was worth the trouble.

Chapter 2

Three Months Later

Charles was at school all day, and Gabrielle was glad because she was tired of him asking if something was wrong with her all morning. Her son was like her personal empath, so connected to her emotions and feelings and always wanting to make things better. She'd never given him that responsibility, but her son took it upon himself to try.

Of course, she lied, but that was because she knew the symptoms and cursed Oliver internally. She should have been suspicious of the large deposit in her account after their secondary one nightstand.

Gabrielle was unwell almost every day, and if she didn't get to her doctor today, she knew she'd never take another day off from the hospital.

Gabrielle pulled up in front of the small private practice. She'd finagled her way to get this appointment with Dr. Chance Jefferson, one of the best obstetricians in Detroit, especially when it came to extraordinary cases.

Damn Oliver. She had a feeling he had done this on purpose.

And she had fallen yet again for his aural manipulation.

Dammit! Why hadn't she reached for the condoms in her side drawer? Any other man, she was making sure, but Oliver... he got in her soul like no other.

Two hours later, Gabrielle was sitting back in her car after the doctor told her the news she already knew.

Leaning her head against the steering column, she knew she would need Oliver's help. Getting sick and trying to stay employed was not going to work.

After the large deposit, Gabrielle had not received any money from Oliver. Payments to the monthly deposits for

Charles' account hadn't dropped either. She had started to use that money to pay off her son's college expenses; instead of waiting for the grants and scholarships to start pouring in at the end of the winter semester. Charles began in early spring.

No matter what, Gabrielle wasn't going to touch her son's savings for personal expenses.

Taking out a notebook, she calculated her expenses. She would need to take at least six months to have the baby, recover and situate her household. At the same time, Charles would be taking his finals and would need emotional support. It would be his first collegiate finals, and she wanted to be there for her son.

She could take money from her retirement to sustain her apartment, but it wouldn't help take care of the baby and all the expenses which went along with that endeavor.

It would become a worse situation if she waited until the last minute.

Pride before the storm, she remembered Oliver's words.

And he did enjoy seeing people squirm.

Maybe he wanted to see her squirm finally.

***

"Mom, are you okay?" Charles asked on the other side of the bathroom door.

He had a right to ask. Gabrielle had been in there for the past hour, trying to cry silently.

Two weeks!

For two weeks, she had been trying to reach Oliver to no avail. Calling his office to ask for him and being constantly told he wasn't there was becoming frustrating. She resorted to spending money searching to find his home address outside of Deckerville, Michigan, a resort town. There was a phone number, but Gabrielle only called twice and hung up when no one answered that sounded even close to Oliver.

There were random emails she tried to reach him through and even his company's contact form. None of this had gotten him to call her back. She probably sounded like a crazy woman to the webmaster.

She resorted to calling her mother to watch Charles.

Ingrid agreed not only because she did seem to dote on her grandson and love him more than she had ever loved Gabrielle, but also because Gabrielle paid her mother fifty dollars. Her mother's boyfriends all seemed to disappear the older Ingrid became, and living off of the small social security she received barely got her through anything in the tiny one-bedroom apartment. Her mother even had the gall to ask Gabrielle if she could move into her apartment to HELP her save money.

Gabrielle had not been a pushover and told her mother no but knew dangling fifty bucks in front of her mother to properly watch Charles, make sure he was fed, and put to bed on time was good enough for Ingrid.

Oliver's house was a two-hour drive from Detroit, Michigan, and on a massive piece of land. Gabrielle looked down at the notebook, opened to a circled monetary amount.

Thirty-thousand dollars.

The gate around the area looked like it cost at least fifty thousand, and she didn't even want to guesstimate the monthly land upkeep; A grand or more, easily. She wasn't familiar with wealth expenses or wanted to be.

A long dark Mercedes limousine passed her slowly with the darkest windows and pulled up in the driveway. There was a box at the gate's entrance, and whoever was in the car pressed a button, and the gate opened.

As tactical as Gabrielle was, a significant unknown factor in her plan was whether Oliver would give her what she needed. He'd be pissed as hell showing up at his home unannounced, but this pregnancy was very unplanned. She had suspected Oliver had every intention of getting her pregnant again, but she would have never suspected he would give her money for a second pregnancy.

Albeit he was drunk all the time, Oliver was intelligent enough to wrap up and not get just anyone pregnant. Gabrielle would ask him instead of dancing around the subject for the money.

Indeed, showing up at his door unannounced pregnant would incense him. He would probably deny he knew her and have her escorted off the property.

Alone, Oliver was a pushover with her, but she never had the pleasure of being with him out in public. From the stories he'd told her, any personal relationships with a black woman would not be favored in any way in his world, and he had his father's reputation to uphold. That whole scenario made him miserable, but he felt it was his obligation to abide.

After sending her location to Ingrid's cell phone, she called her mother.

"What's this?" Ingrid questioned.

"That's where I am."

"Who's this? I can't see anything on Google. It's just a field."

"I need to be here, but if you don't hear from me by tonight, can you call the police?"

Ingrid grunted. "Ain't nothing worth being killed, Gabby. Come home. You got responsibilities."

"I'm doing this because I have responsibilities, Ingrid." She huffed because being compared to her mother always begging men for money just irritated her soul, and Gabrielle was tempted to drive back to Detroit. Still, the butterflies in her stomach were the baby's anxiousness. Putting her hand on her belly to calm herself, she said, "I know you don't care, but I just needed you to know where to find the body."

She hung up because taking any advice from Ingrid, who only cared about herself, was just stupid. Touching the side of her face remembering the slaps Ingrid had viciously delivered, started to upset her.

Once Gabrielle received the money, she wouldn't have to deal with Ingrid anymore. She'd have enough to get back on her feet, take care of Charles even, and adequately take care of the new baby. By next year, she'd have her job back or would be able to get any other position with just as much pay.

A surgical assistant was a lucrative position, but one had to be at the top of their game if they wanted to work in the place.

Currently, she wasn't at the top of her game, and even her doctor had deemed her high risk. In so many words, he said she needed to sit her butt down and rest if she didn't want to lose the baby.

Putting the car in drive, Gabrielle pulled up to the box and pressed the green button.

"I'm here to see Oliver...F-Farnsworth." She faltered because she had never said his full name out loud.

"Who is this?" a woman's voice sharply demanded.

"My name is Gabrielle Payne."

"What do you want?"

Gabrielle almost said something sarcastic. Taking a deep breath, she said, "I'm looking for Oliver Farnsworth. I need to tell him something very important."

There was a long silence on the other line. So long, Gabrielle was about to push the green button again for service.

"You can come around back to the service entrance," the women came back.

She glared at the box in pure frustration. "Look, lady, I need to speak with Oliver. Is he here or not?"

There was another long pause before a man came after and said sharply. "Oliver's not here, so get your trifling ass off the property."

She didn't care about respecting Oliver's family at this point, but she needed to get to Oliver. "I've been trying to reach him for two weeks, and it's important I speak with him concerning a dire situation."

"What is your name?" the man asked as if she hadn't said it.

"GAB-BRI-ELLE-PAYNE!" She enunciated loudly.

There was yet another moment of silence.

Laying her head, vexing on the steering wheel, she was about to give up and drive away until the initial woman's voice came on the speaker. "What's your phone number?"

This was a strange question, but she slowly rattled off her phone number.

After another minute, the gates opened.

Gabrielle hesitated because why was her phone number significant after everything they had just put her through.

Driving up to the front of the house, she got out of the car and looked at the large two-story 21st Century palatial home. The front doors were about fifty feet from the driveway, and Gabrielle hiked herself up there as the red front door opened.

A woman dressed in black came out. Gabrielle walked closer, noting the Arabic older features were prominent along with the disdain on her face. The woman couldn't be more than five foot one, whereas Gabrielle felt she towered above this woman at five foot five. Her dark hair, dark eyes, and small features placed her at least over sixty, as she looked over circle rimmed glasses like she couldn't believe Gabrielle's audacity of coming in the vicinity of the property.

"How can I help you, Gabrielle Payne?" the older woman asked stiffly.

It was November, and the crisp Michigan Huron Lake air whipped about them briskly. Gabrielle was dressed for outside, but this woman wasn't. Yet, Gabrielle knew this woman would die before she allowed a black woman to come through the front doors as a welcomed guest.

"I told you how you can help me. I need to speak with Oliver, so if you could call him and just let him know I'm here, I don't mind waiting in my car."

The woman looked past Gabrielle at the vehicle parked in front of the home, and her face grew even more contentious. "And you were told Oliver is not here-"

Gabrielle cut her off. "I have been trying to locate him for the past two weeks unsuccessfully, and I'm just trying to get a message to him."

"You can tell me the message," the woman insisted.

"I won't," she sneered through gritted teeth. "Just get Oliver on the phone and tell him I'm here, plus-lease." Not wanting to be another minute in front of this small Arabic General, Gabrielle walked off the porch and went to sit in her vehicle.

The woman hurriedly went to the doorway and called someone.

Gabrielle knew it was probably to get her kicked off the property. Yes, she had lost her temper, but this woman... whoever she was, deserved something even worse.

"A sock in the nose!" Oliver would have suggested because he knew Gabrielle would never resort to violence. "Or would you sarcasm them to death, Gabrielle?"

He always had a way to say the most ridiculous thing to make her laugh.

Whomever, the woman, called finally came to the door. It was a man. He was taller than the older woman, but since Gabrielle was parked so damn far from the door, she couldn't make out the features.

Getting out of the car, hoping to confront the man as he walked brusquely towards her, she prepared to blurt out she was pregnant because she felt it was the only thing that would get results.

Oliver would have to be angry later, but she needed to get home, and these people just needed to give her the respect of Oliver's baby mother or get ready for a verbal cursing she would lay upon them.

Tightening her coat and then approaching the man as he advanced on her, Gabrielle looked up into his face to announce her pregnancy until she noticed the gray-tannish eyes glaring at her.

Gabrielle tripped over her own feet and fell face forward, but the man was close enough to catch her.

"Oliver," she cried, relieved, throwing her arms around his neck. "Oh my god, Oliver. I've been trying to reach you."

The man continued to glare heatedly at her and was about to say something, but she didn't want him to get a word in to yell at her, so she spoke at the same time he spoke.

"I'm pregnant!" she announced.

He snarled, "I'm not Oliver."

THE TROUBLE WITH GABRIELLE

Chapter 3

You're Who?! You're What?!

Before they acknowledged what they had revealed, they both realized they were still holding onto each other at the exact moment.

She scrambled away from him and righted herself to look up into familiar eyes, not understanding how this looked like Oliver, but it wasn't. This man had Oliver's face but swarthiness, carrying a light beard and mustache on his jaw, thicker and slightly longer hair. He possessed the true gorgeousness she always wished for Oliver, but the drugs and alcohol had stolen.

Not this guy. He was what Oliver should have looked like if Oliver had stayed away from chemicals.

The man stood up and stepped two feet away from her.

"I'm David Farnsworth," he corrected her.

"You're a twin?" she questioned.

"He doesn't like ... Oliver didn't like to acknowledge me as a twin, so I'm used to people being shocked." He looked down at her stomach skeptically. "You're pregnant? By whom?"

Straightening her spine, she said, "Oliver. Almost four months."

He narrowed his eyes again, clearly showing he thought he was lying. "You're not Oliver's type," David said.

"How would you know Oliver's type when he never spoke to you about what he liked?" she asked, standing akimbo. "Matter of fact, you're the last person Oliver would talk to about anything he liked."

Again, his eyes narrowed, but this time it was different. He was accessing her. Oliver would do that when he thought she wasn't looking as if trying to read her mind.

"Come in, Ms. Payne," he said, opening his arms and aiming his hand towards the door. "It's cold. You can't sit in your car."

Gabrielle looked at the house where the general woman still stood. By now, the woman was showing how cold she was by hugging herself, but she didn't move from the front door.

"Nah," Gabrielle said. "I'll wait in the car for Oliver."

"If you're just here for some money, you came at the wrong time. You're not getting a dime."

"That matter is between Oliver and me," she said, not wanting to discuss this matter with someone who had been Oliver's nemesis.

David said disgustedly, "Oliver will want nothing from you."

"Most likely, but he'll take care of his responsibility."

"How do you even know it's his?" he snarled. "You look like you get around - a lot."

Gabrielle tightened her fist, but dammit, she wasn't a physically violent person, but this guy was pushing her to the edge. "Even if I were easy and horny as a devil, I wouldn't give you the time of day, David Farnsworth. And I'm certainly not about to stand here and have a battle of wits with an unarmed person. I'll wait for Oliver in the car."

"No, you won't," David said. "You'll get the fuck off this property and never even think about this place or Oliver ever again."

"Oliver would want to know about this baby, so you better be a good little boy for once and go call him," she said in her most condescending tone, knowing she was pissing him off.

The man grimaced. "No, I won't. And neither will anyone else call him for you, Ms. Payne, no matter how much you insist."

His proximity was doing a number on her equilibrium, but she braved stepping close to him to make him uncomfortable. He stepped away.

Smirking, she said, "Don't worry, David. You couldn't get anything from me no matter how hard you tried. Intermittent impotence from your condition must be frustrating."

"Why would Oliver tell all his business to a woman like you? What did you blackmail him with?"

She cackled insanely. "I didn't have to blackmail or threaten Oliver." Knowing sex was a sore point with David, she said, "Oliver never denied me with anything, even in bed." Sighing as if she hadn't just dug invisible nails into his soul, she pronounced stubbornly, "He's going to come home eventually tonight, and I can wait as well." Gabrielle started to turn around to go to her car because she just wanted to get away from David. She knew she'd never stop staring at him if she didn't.

Oliver most likely didn't tell her about David or show her a picture because he knew its effect on her. There was no secret she told Oliver he looked very handsome. They were honest with each other, and most likely, he suspected if she saw David, she'd only have eyes for him.

David followed her and reached in his pants pocket to take out a burgundy cell phone. Oliver's favorite color.

Gabrielle stopped in her tracks, realizing it was Oliver's phone.

She remembered when he had taken it out to check some messages before he left that last morning. He'd also put in Charles' birthday on his calendar. She thought it had been strange for him to ask about his son's birthday when he never cared before. Oliver had never sent Charles a birthday present or ever changed the payment amount to recognize the day Charles was born.

Forgetting her attraction to David's face, Gabrielle walked up to him and reached out for the phone. David pulled it away from her, and she was forced to look up at him.

"Why doesn't he have his phone?" she demanded.

"Because he doesn't need it anymore, Ms. Payne."

She frowned, not understanding what he meant. "What do you mean?"

"Oliver's dead," David hissed out.

The world seemed to whirl around her like a carousel ride for a moment, and she was glad the back of the car was behind her because as she stumbled back, the back of her thighs hit the hood and caught her. At least the car was warm enough for her to lean on, and she gripped her chest with one hand and held her stomach with the other.

"No," she said pathetically as if just that one word could make the sentence he spoke untrue. "H-How? When? He was just... we were just...."

"Lies, Ms. Payne. Oliver died three months ago. Shortly after a business trip from Detroit to drum up more business...." His voice trailed off. "When did you see him?"

"August nineteenth in Detroit," she answered, not caring if he believed her or not. "I remember because my son was taking his entrance exam to college."

David frowned. "And he came to see you?"

She could feel uncontrollable tears stream down her cheek, almost freezing on her face. "H-He stayed the night." It was hard for her to swallow because she wanted to scream. "He's really dead?"

"He died of a heart attack a month after returning."

It was now too disturbing to look at him, so she stared at the ground and started to ask, "Did he... I guess not since you didn't know who I was."

"We buried him today," David offered. "Yet, as I said, you're not Oliver's type. We knew the vultures would come out but not this soon."

Gabrielle couldn't stay there, and she certainly couldn't ask them for money!

As she started to get into her car, she caught sight of the notebook still on the front passenger seat, with the circled amount.

And then she heard Oliver saying, "Pride before the storm."

Keeping her eyes down to the ground, she said, "I still need money. To get me over until I have the baby. That's all I was going to ask him for." Grabbing the notebook, she handed it to David to show she had thought about the amount carefully.

David scoffed. "And in a month, you'll be back for more and more. It will never end. Do you think I'm stupid enough to believe Oliver would make you pregnant? Do you know how many paternity suits he fought off? I know because he loved telling me how some woman pretended to be pregnant and how I'll never know the feeling of any woman ever having that pleasure. Oliver took great lengths to make sure he never impregnated anyone. It would shame our entire family, and I know he would never have sex with someone like you. Never. Stop wasting our fucking time and yours with these false claims. If you are pregnant, it's certainly not by Oliver."

His words hurt, but Gabrielle had the truth behind her. "The amount is not going to destitute your family. I'll take any test to prove it's Oliver's, but I need the money in less than a month, or I won't be able to pay any bills."

He snatched the notebook and flung it over the car. "GET THE FUCK OFF THIS PROPERTY, YOU STUPID ASS BLACK BITCH!"

Gabrielle's fist clenched again, but her voice was deceptively calm as she said, "Oliver was right. You ARE more horrible."

Going around the car to pick up the notebook, she let the tears flow and not caring if this man saw her anguish and despair. When she came around to sit in the car, she noticed the flask Oliver left at her home had fallen out of her coat pocket. It was useless, so she tossed it on the dashboard to get it out of her way before sitting in the car and closing the door.

David walked up to the car and said something while she cranked up her loud vehicle that was in desperate need of a muffler.

She faintly heard him speaking, but since she couldn't look at his familiar face without feeling miserable, Gabrielle proceeded to put the car in reverse until David hit the windshield so hard he cracked the glass.

ASSHOLE!

Now she was going to sock him in the face!

THE TROUBLE WITH GABRIELLE

CHAPTER 4

SHOULD SHE STAY OR SHOULD SHE GO?

Gabrielle probably looked ridiculous, but she didn't bother to put the car in park. Red seething anger enveloped her, making her jump from the vehicle and run at David full force to shove him to the ground. She heard a crash, but she was so hell-bent on jumping on top of him, trying to scratch his eyes out.

He grabbed her wrist, rolled them over until he was above her, screaming for her to stop, but she wouldn't!

Gabrielle didn't! She wanted to see blood. She wanted to see his perfect mouth ripped off, and that rugged jawline scratched over and his eyes - GONE! She wanted those torn out of their socket and flung around like he had done her notebook.

David shook her so hard against the ground he temporarily knocked the breath from her.

There were sirens in the distance, and she smelled smoke, but she was so paralyzed she couldn't move for a long moment.

David leaned over her in concern and called her by her first name in a concerned gentle tone. She closed her eyes when he called her again. Damn, why'd he have to sound like Oliver?

"Gabrielle, say something," David pleaded, leaning down to press his ear to her nose. To someone else, he said, "I don't think she's breathing."

Suddenly, she felt his cold hand on her hot chest, but that didn't bother her. His touch brought her back to reality.

Looking down to his hand under her shirt, she gasped and slapped him as hard as she could across his face before scrambling up. "You pervert," she seethed.

David held his hand by the wrist as if he was going to cut it off. "I'm sorry. I couldn't tell if you were breathing."

She looked around for her car and gasped. Remembering she hadn't put it in park, the vehicle had continued backward and crashed into a tree, which somehow ignited the gas tank, AND caught the entire car on fire.

Falling to the ground, Gabrielle sobbed in misery. No car meant an even worse fate if she didn't get any money. Burying her face in her hands, she cried, "No! No! No!"

How could this be happening to her?

What the hell was she supposed to do?

"Ms. Payne," David said with a lot of fear in his voice. "Please come to the house and rest. We'll find you a car service to take you home."

She looked back at her car, miserable, but didn't move. In deep thought, her hand rested on her chin as she stared at the flames. Someone must've called the police and fire because they were there already as if they lived right around the corner from this address.

The fire department was putting out the flames, and the cop was coming over to say something to her.

"Little girl," the sheriff snapped two fingers in front of her eyes.

Unable to say anything, she pulled her head back to look at him.

"She must be some crackhead," the sheriff determined, taking his cuffs out.

Behind her, some woman shouted, "Arrest her! Arrest her now!"

The sheriff grabbed Gabrielle by the shoulder, viciously yanking her up, and started to slap the cuffs on her. Suddenly the fight returned, and she tried to wrench from the officer's grip.

"Get your hands off me," Gabrielle screamed.

David halted the officer. "Wait! Please, she's in shock. She's not high," he said. "She just found out my brother died, officer. We'll take care of her. And let me know any charges, please."

The sheriff looked reluctant to release her like he'd caught a big fish. "You sure about that, Mr. Farnsworth. We can hold her until you press charges."

"We aren't pressing charges," David said.

"Yes, we are," the small woman screamed, finally coming upon them at arm's length. "She caused damage to our property, she attacked you, David, and she's on drugs."

The sheriff started to reach for Gabrielle again, but David pulled her behind his body for protection.

"All of that is a lie, sir. I made her lose control of her car when I broke her windshield, and I called her a name... well, you know, and she's not on drugs. We'll take care of her," David assured the officer.

Warily the sheriff tore his eyes from Gabrielle and walked to the fire scene.

Gabrielle figured the fat white man was relaying David's decision not to charge her and leave the scene.

David turned to her with that glare, but the man was so damn fine she wasn't trying to stare up at him.

"I-I can get home on my own," she said because there was no way in hell she was going in that house with this man. "Just... Please think about the money and call me. My number's in Oliver's phone."

She tried to walk around David, still staring at his feet, but he moved to block her path. "I have too many questions for you, Ms. Payne."

"No," she said, shaking her head. "Not tonight. I gotta..." She wanted to cry again. Oliver was dead! Oliver was dead! Her brain screamed.

Again, she tried to go around him, but David moved smoothly.

"Please, Gabrielle."

Looking up in his face again, instantly mesmerized by those damn gorgeous eyes." Fine," she said. "Just until I can... I can find a way h-home." Her voice trembled.

David walked towards the house but occasionally looked back to see if she followed.

Slowly she dragged her feet, looking at the back of his shoes. If she didn't look at him, she could forget how devilishly handsome he was, but what about when he spoke softly... like Oliver.

Damn!

Reaching in her pockets, she felt relief feeling her phone.

"Ms. Payne," a firefighter called for her.

She stopped and turned back to the wreckage of her car. They'd gotten the fire out, but the smoke billowed in the sky, disappearing in the clouds like her hopes and dreams.

David came back beside her as if to protect her from the first responder.

The firefighter carried some items from the car that were salvaged. "These came from the car and looked valuable. And we found your purse in the back seat on the floor intact."

He gave her the large purse, an almost burnt notebook, and the flask.

The tiny older Arab woman came beside them. "That's Oliver's!" she exclaimed. "You stole that from him!"

Pressing the flask to her chest, Gabrielle said sorrowfully, "He left it at my house."

David said something to the woman in another language sharply. The woman wanted to say something but didn't. Instead, the older woman stormed away into the house. David thanked the firefighter and then said to Gabrielle, "Please join us for dinner while you wait for the car service."

Gabrielle only looked at the ground and continued to follow him.

When she got to the first step of the home, she stopped. David paused at the red door and turned around to watch her.

She didn't have to look up to his face to see what he was doing. Her peripheral vision caught every nuance of this man because her inner attraction was on him like white on rice.

Yet, this was Oliver's home, and David was Oliver's brother. Neither one of them Oliver would want her to get anywhere near.

But she was here at Oliver's home, and she was ten feet away from his brother.

"Gabrielle?" David called out.

Ignoring him, she knelt and pressed her hand on the cold concrete. Oliver had lived here. He had called this place home even though he seemed to feel safe and secure when he was with her.

Closing her eyes, she prepared herself to walk into Oliver's house. She would stay just for a moment because she knew she couldn't hold her peace as Oliver could.

Standing back up, Gabrielle stepped up on the porch and walked to the red door where David still stood.

"Oliver wasn't a nice person," David said.

"I know," she said, only going as far as the top of his tie. "He told me all the time he was a horrible person, but the Oliver shown to me was a man you will never know." She smiled, feeling triumphant knowing Oliver had given her that secret.

"Would you prove you're pregnant?" he asked.

"How?"

He pointed to a door a few steps across from the front door. "There's a guest bathroom. My stepsister has put a pregnancy kit in there for you. It's new. Unopened. She just got them. We ask you to take the test and bring the stick out so we can see the results together to prove you are pregnant."

Gabrielle could fully understand their doubt. A stranger showing up at their door proclaiming to be pregnant seemed highly suspicious, but she wasn't going to be cordial about it. "Even if I take the test, it doesn't prove it's Oliver's."

"But at least it will prove you aren't lying about a pregnancy. We help you thinking you're carrying my brother's child and then find out three months, you run off with my stepmother's generosity." David looks bitter. "He's had too many paternity suits and Neema doesn't need to be hurt any more."

31

As she proceeded to the bathroom, he blocked her for a second. "I need to take your items. I wouldn't want them to hamper you."

Narrowing her eyes, she knew he suspected she could have something in her purse to manipulate the test. Before giving her purse to David, she put the flask and notebook in her purse and zipped her bag closed. She warned, "If you guys go through and take any of MY stuff, I'm pressing charges."

Going into the bathroom, Gabrielle opened the sealed kit and proceeded to pee on the electronic stick.

After flushing the toilet, she gasped at herself, seeing herself in the mirror. She looked like a hot fat mess! Dirt splotches were all over her face, her eyeliner had run down her face making her look like a sad, dark clown, and the matte lipstick was smeared all over her chin and cheeks.

Her natural had dried out, and the curls had tightened up, and she wasn't even going to examine the damage to her clothes.

Gabrielle cleaned herself up and came out of the bathroom, where David stood like a guard by the door. She handed him the stick just as it beeped with the results, and he returned her purse to her.

Immediately, Gabrielle pulled the flask out of the purse and pulled that to her chest glad they had not taken this away.

David had watched her and she noted he looked jealousy down at the flask for a moment.

"Don't you want to see the results?" he asked nervously.

"I don't have to see the results when I already know what it's going to say."

David looked down at the stick and took a deep breath. "You're pregnant," he said as if he were giving her the news for the first time.

"Hurry up and get the car here, David," Gabrielle ordered. "I'll sign whatever you want me to sign to get the money and never come back. I don't want to be here any longer than I have to be."

Walking past David into the expansive hall, she felt renewed, strong, and confident she'd be able to get through this.

Whether they gave her the money or not, Gabrielle was here, and she'd be home with her son soon.

This family, which had made Oliver very miserable, would figure something out, but she was almost at the point of not caring about the outcome. Gabrielle just wanted to get away from here as fast as possible.

THE TROUBLE WITH GABRIELLE

CHAPTER 5

THE DAY SHE MET HIM!

The smell of cooked, roasted garlic wafted in through her nose, and her stomach loudly growled. Gabrielle hadn't eaten since early that morning, and even then, it had been just a half-eaten saltine and water. The baby took morning sickness to another level, and anything heavier took her to back-breaking convulsions over a toilet until the afternoon.

"We were about to sit down and eat," David said. "May I take your-"

Gabrielle cut him off, refusing his offer, "No."

He walked down a hallway, and she followed him closely but still maintained no further eye contact than his Achilles heel. He turned into a large open room, and she realized the hallway ran along the rest of the house that opened up into a stream of other large spaces. This doorway opened into the dining room part with enough for eight people to comfortably sit down and eat.

Only two other people were in the room. The evil older Arabic woman and a mini version of her still had a stern look but seemed to mask most of her real emotions. She was dressed in black, completely covered from head to toe, including a scarf to cover her hair.

Gabrielle wasn't an idiot. A black woman wasn't welcome here. So many times Oliver reminded her how illicit their relationship had been and how his family would have rebuffed him if he dared reveal her to anyone.

Had.

That thought lingered for a moment sending her hand under her chin for comfort to rub softly.

"Why'd you need my phone number?" Gabrielle inquired to the room.

David looked at the older woman and then at the younger woman.

No one looked like they wanted to answer.

Huffing in irritation and folding her arms over her chest, Gabrielle snipped, "Any day now."

The young woman forced herself to smile. 'I'm Mina McGee," she introduced. "For months, we've been trying to figure out Oliver's private safe. It was unbreakable, and according to the lawyer, the will is in there. When we get to the will, we can put all the financial matters to rest. Oliver didn't leave the combination with anyone." She walked a little closer to Gabrielle. "Your nine-digit phone number opened the first safe."

"The first one?"

David spoke. "There are two more. Just as secure."

Gabrielle turned away from him, standing closer to the woman, and looked over the table of food. Her stomach was crying. The food smelled delicious.

"This is from the repast we had this morning," David explained. "We have more than enough."

"Is the car service going to be here soon?" Gabrielle asked sharply, still not looking at him.

"Soon," David assured her.

Looking at the young woman, Gabrielle questioned, "Did you get the other safes open?"

"No," she admitted. "We cannot figure out what Oliver used."

"But you could," David said encouragingly.

Rolling her eyes, she said, slightly turning to him. "And hell could freeze over before I help you out, David."

David seemed shocked by her animosity. "If you're asking for an apology, Ms. Payne, then I give it."

She turned all the way around to him and forgot how damn handsome he was. David inherited all the good things from Oliver, but he exuded this sexuality like pollen to a bee. Her sex responded like a four-year-old happy about Christmas coming, and it was difficult not to feel amorous all over just from looking at Oliver's brother.

"Don't be nice now, David. I was a stupid ass black bitch just a few minutes ago."

"I've apologized," he said stiffly.

"What was in the initial safe other than more safes?" she asked Mina turning away from David.

"None of your business," Neema snipped.

"Then I can wait by the door for my car," she said and started to turn around, but Mina gasped.

"Please, don't. Please sit and eat with us." She looked over at David with a nod, who immediately left the room.

Now that David wasn't around, Gabrielle felt a little more comfortable in her skin and could think clearly. Sitting down at the chair offered by Mina, she looked down at Neema, who was staring more at the flask than at Gabrielle. The other end was set up most likely for David, and she was glad she sat a chair away from that end. Hooking her purse on the back of her chair, she put the flask between her legs to hold securely.

"He never left that anywhere," Neema said, narrowing her dark eyes. "It belonged to his grandfather on his mother's side."

Gabrielle responded, "I figured he was going to come back for it, but he didn't. He didn't call for it or come by again."

Mina fixed Gabrielle's plate and then sat on the other side of the table from Gabrielle. "Can I know how you two met?" she asked, trying to lighten the mood in the room as she placed a napkin in her lap.

David returned with an odd size steel box about as large as a massive dictionary. Sitting at the other end of the table, Gabrielle noticed he nodded at Mina about something.

Feeling out of sorts because she didn't know the proper etiquette for dinner like this, Gabrielle copied Mina's motions, putting a napkin in her lap.

"He requested me for a job," Gabrielle answered evasively, knowing David was watching every word she spoke. "And then asked me to stay. I didn't realize until after he was gone I was pregnant, but I have a feeling Oliver knew he'd gotten me pregnant because a couple of weeks after I started having symptoms, he sent a large amount of money to my bank account."

"His father was like that," Neema admitted. "He knew I was pregnant, but I lost the baby."

"How many months pregnant?" Mina questioned.

"Almost four." Gabrielle picked through her potatoes and ate some bread. It was going farther into the evening, which meant it was getting closer to the morning, and she didn't feel like looking at this in the commode from her stomach. There was some chicken roasted in some red sauce and a green vegetable she couldn't identify, but it smelled delicious. She tasted it just a little and then looked at her watch.

"How long until that car?" she questioned David but didn't look at him.

"Soon," he answered again.

Gabrielle felt she wouldn't get anything from him, especially money before she left, so she decided to put her offer to the whole table. "Look, I only came because Oliver was taking care of his responsibility, and then he stopped. Now that I'm very high risk, I'm unable to work for about six months. I'm here to ask for thirty thousand dollars. That's enough to have the baby, situate my household and then get back to work. That's all I need. I'm able to sustain myself and my family, and I will not ask for anything else."

David started to say something, but Mina held up a hand to him and said to Gabrielle, "Will you sign over papers to attest you won't ask for another dime?"

"Yes, as long as you sign papers over releasing any hold over me or my child," she stated.

"No," David said adamantly. "If this is Oliver's child, we have just as much right to influence him as you do. Oliver would have wanted that."

She remembered Oliver's words about David not being able to have kids. "I'm not some surrogate birthing center to offset your need for children, David. Just because you and your wife couldn't muster a single brat doesn't mean I'm responsible for helping you get through an unfulfilled life."

He shot out of his seat, and so did she, ready to do battle with him. Getting him angry seemed the only way she could ensure she didn't show her attraction to him.

"Please!" Mina said. "This is a very emotional day for all of us. David, it does no good to get her upset."

"You can't tell me to get the fuck out one minute and then want me the next minute," Gabrielle seethed.

"I don't want you," David said disgustedly and looked down at her stomach.

Protectively, she put her arms around her stomach. "You are not taking my baby," she stated. "Oliver would have let me raise it."

"You don't know that," David said.

She did, but she wasn't going to tell him how she knew this.

Mina looked down at David and nodded at the steel box. He brought the box to her, and Mina put the steel box in the middle of the table in front of Gabrielle. "This is the second safe."

"Why is this all important to get into Oliver's stuff? Wouldn't the executor of his will be in charge of this? Or whoever inherited his estate?" Gabrielle questioned.

"Yes," Mina said. "But the lawyer over Oliver's estate said everything we need to answer those questions along with the will would be in Oliver's safe. Until then, the estate is in flux, but a generous amount has been set aside for the upkeep of everything Oliver owns and to keep the business running."

"And who is running the business now?" Gabrielle asked distastefully, glaring.

"Until we can get a hold of the will, my mother serves as a temporary proxy over everything for the next year since she was married to Oliver's father," Mina explained. "With Oliver not having any children that we knew of, my mother is the rightful heir. We started a guardianship case to extend until my mother's lifetime."

Gabrielle straightened up and smiled, sitting back down. "But now?"

"If the child proves to be Oliver's, there's no doubt he or she will inherit the estate and the business because David can't," Neema said.

"I don't want it," Gabrielle said stubbornly.

"Liar," David snarled. "You came here for pennies."

"I came here to sustain my life until I can get back to work. My pregnancy keeps me from working, and just like I told Oliver, I don't want his support."

"But he gave it anyway?" David asked incredulously.

"He found my bank account number somehow and dropped the money in there like clockwork until... Well, until he stopped." Looking at her watch, Gabrielle said, "I need to make a phone call and also charge my phone while I wait for the car."

Leaning over the table as if to intimidate her, David ordered, "We need you to open the box, Ms. Payne."

She laughed at his threatening visage.

"What's so funny?" he demanded to know.

"People in hell need water, David. You need me, and I need you. I think we've come to a standoff." Frowning, she looked at the small electrical lock requesting eight digits. "Why would I know the lock combination?"

David put his hand on Mina's shoulder, and Gabrielle noted how the woman laid her hand on top of his. Were they closer than what was presumed?

"Like we said," Mina said with a tight calmness. "Your phone number opened the first safe, and most likely, all the other locks have to do with you. Any tampering of the locks destroys what's inside each safe."

"And you can't do shit without the will, right?" Gabrielle determined.

"You have a dirty mouth," David said in disdain.

"So do you," she countered.

"I have no idea what my brother saw in you. You're nasty, ugly, and ghetto."

Mina squeezed on David's hand, reminding him, "David, she needs something from us, and we need something from her."

Gabrielle smirked. "You're right. I do." Sliding the steel box in front of her, she looked at the top. Engraved was something in another language.

"It's Hindu," Neema said.

"What does it mean?" Gabrielle questioned.

Neema looked at David, who answered, "Pain in my Heart."

Gabrielle smiled and ran her fingers over the letters lovingly.

Mina gasped. "It's you. Your last name is Payne."

Knowingly, she nodded and pulled the box closer. This was just for her. Oliver had made sure only she could open this box and the digits needed were most likely a date only she would know, but it wouldn't be evident to others... the day they met. "May I open it in private? In Oliver's room."

"You don't know the combination," David said.

She put in the eight digits, and the green light clicked on the lock, but when David reached for it, Gabrielle quickly turned all the numbers so the combination would lock again.

His angry visage returned, but she only smiled.

"If we all are going to play crazy, I play with a full deck, David," she said with triumph.

They messed with the wrong one tonight.

THE TROUBLE WITH GABRIELLE

Chapter 6

Oliver Was Right!

Coolly, she pointed out, "I'm not stupid, David. And I knew Oliver a little bit better than you think. If he used my phone number for the initial safe, I figured he would use something else about me."

"Your birthday?" Mina guessed.

Gabrielle shook her head. "The day we met. Now can I please have somewhere private I can make a call?"

"I will show her," Neema insisted.

Gabrielle followed her out of the room, not giving David another look, but she could feel his eyes driving into her back where he probably wanted to jam a knife.

With Neema alone and a little bit cordial, Gabrielle asked, "I'm not trying to be rude, but what did Oliver die of?"

"A heart attack."

That death didn't sit right with Gabrielle. "Did he have a history of heart disease?"

Neema shrugged. "My guess would be as good as yours, Ms. Payne. Oliver kept many secrets. You are one we never expected."

They went up two flights of stairs to get to the second level, which opened to another long hallway, but this time with bedrooms on each side and at the end double doors. "We didn't know whether Oliver was coming and going with his depression and refusal to take any medication."

Gabrielle frowned because she clearly remembered despite Oliver's drunkenness, he was adamant about not taking any medication.

Before entering the room, Neema turned to Gabrielle and asked, "Is it his? Are you carrying his child, Ms. Payne?"

"Yes, I wouldn't come this way all by myself to mess with people. I don't have the time or inclination to cause harm to people who are grieving. The financial assistance I request will be final. You won't see me anymore. I promise."

"But David won't agree to those terms. You would carry the last of the bloodline. Can't you consider visitations?"

Could she bear having David anywhere near Detroit? He would see Charles and know something was up. "I'll think about it."

Neema turned into a glass opening and led Gabrielle into a massive bedroom with gray tones.

Seeing the cabinet across the room with the open safe and the Hindu art deco, Gabrielle was positive this was Oliver's room. This was his taste.

Neema wrung her fingers in nervousness. "Since I'm temporarily in custody for a moment of Oliver's estate, I would ask if you want the money you need, you stay here and attempt to see David in a better light. Just a few days, please," Neema insisted. "You may have Oliver's room."

"I can't stay!" she said. "I have to get home."

"Why? What responsibilities? You aren't working. You are alone."

"I have a son."

"He's in college, according to David."

She didn't know when David had a chance to tell them all that information, but she didn't want them to know too much about her. If she was going to allow David in her life, the less they knew about her, the better.

"I'll have to call home. Give me a moment. Thank you, ma'am," Gabrielle said, dismissing the woman.

When Neema was gone, Gabrielle figured out how to ensconce herself in the room. The door was a balcony style with frosted glass, and when pulled over the glass doorway, it provided privacy in the room and could even be locked.

She had her charger in her coat and was able to find a wall port where she could plug her cell phone inside. Quickly she called Ingrid to assure her mother she was still alive.

"Are you on your way home?" Ingrid asked tiredly.

"Not yet. I'm waiting on a car. I had an accident."

"See, I told you not to go out there. I knew them white ass people would do something."

"They aren't white, Ingrid."

"It doesn't matter, Gabby. They ain't black, and that means they are on the wrong side."

Gabrielle didn't feel like going in with her mother like this. "How's my son?"

"Sleep," Ingrid said as if it was apparent.

Charles was good about taking care of himself, and the only reason Gabrielle needed Ingrid was to make sure neighbors didn't accuse her of leaving a little boy at home alone.

"Would you be able to stay with him for a few days?"

"Yes, but I'll need some money."

Her mother had agreed just a little bit too fast, but Gabrielle was desperate and would find out her mother's hidden intentions later.

In the background, she heard Charles say, "Is that Momma?"

"You should be in bed, Charles," her mother reprimanded gently.

"I'll talk to him," Gabrielle said.

A second later, Charles said, "I miss you, Momma."

"I miss you too, honey."

"How is everything? Are you okay? Where'd you go?"

Being honest with her son was going to be the only way he was assured she was alright. "I went to see a friend, but I was too late. He died."

"I'm sorry," Charles said with sympathy. "What did he die of?"

She wanted to cry hearing her son's concern. "They said he had a heart attack."

"You don't sound like you believe them."

She sometimes forgot how intelligent and empathic her son could be. "I don't. He was healthy, and he had good stamina. He only drank alcohol, but he was five years older than I, with no history."

"Can you get the medical records?" Charles asked. "Maybe looking them over will give you more clarity."

Of course, her son would be thinking of everything she hadn't. "I could, but I was calling to let you know I have to stay away for a couple of days. Afterward, everything will be a million times better."

"I'll keep my phone charged," Charles promised. "Call me for anything."

"Thank you. I love you."

"I love you too, Momma."

Ingrid's voice came back on the line. "Put enough money in my bank account for me and some to buy food for him as soon as possible."

Reluctantly she thanked her mother and hung up. As soon as she got off the phone, Gabrielle went into her bank account and sent money to her mother's account.

Sitting on Oliver's bed, she looked around the room again, taking in an area she never knew about this man. Turning to the pillows, she laid her head down and closed her eyes. She could smell Oliver's shampoo, and she smiled, letting the tears come quickly.

Getting back up, she walked to the large safe and knelt to look at the important papers, and there was some jewelry. She would guesstimate over a million dollars' worth of jewelry, but she didn't touch anything.

Going back to the bed where she had left the steel box, she opened the lock and then opened the box.

The contents didn't look as if they had been there long. On top of the box, Gabrielle saw an envelope for her, and there was an envelope for David, in Oliver's handwriting. Below was another keycode to hide what else was in the box. At least an inch of space was left in the box, and she couldn't imagine what could be in there and when she tried the date again, it didn't work.

Oliver knew she wasn't stupid. He would have made it, so she would have to think about it.

The bathroom door opened abruptly, and she jumped up from the bed.

David stood there but didn't fully enter the room. "I thought you should know this is a shared bathroom between these two bedrooms."

"Who's bedroom?"

"Mine."

Damn, why did that sound so possessive.

"We've shared the bathroom since we were young."

"Is there another bedroom I can have?"

"I'm not going to hurt you," David said sourly. "You can lock the door to my side when you go in. Mina has the bedroom across the hall for now, and Neema has the one across from mine. The master bedroom has become more of a shrine to my father. Neema never felt comfortable sleeping in after he passed away, and then they were going to change it over to a nursery, while Mina moved into mine after she married Oliver."

"Wait... what? Oliver was going to marry Mina?"

"Oh, there's something you don't know about Oliver?" He looked surprised.

"That's his step-sister," Gabrielle pointed out.

"It's not a blood relation."

"But morally, it's wrong. I see why Oliver drunk all the time. The dilemma he must've been in."

"You speak of morals as a prostitute?" David questioned. "No matter, Ms. Payne, when Oliver came back from Detroit, he suddenly changed his mind about marrying Mina and refused. He said he wouldn't."

"Mina must've been devastated."

"It wasn't a love union. Her husband died a long time ago, and she hasn't had any children. It would have been more convenient."

"Hence the separate rooms?"

"According to Mina, Oliver insisted when the idea of marrying her was initially proposed," David explained. "May I come in?"

She noticed he was still at the bathroom doorway and was impressed he was respecting her space. "Yes."

He walked several steps into the room. "I hold a lot of frustration about my brother, and I know I have been rude and racist towards you tonight, Ms. Payne. I hope you understand and truly accept my apology."

Chapter 7

Can He Touch You?

Gabrielle could feel his earnestness, and from everything Oliver told her about this family, especially David, she could understand the man's frustration. Oliver had wasted his life to a life David would have loved. And Gabrielle held their bloodline in more ways than one, but they'd never know about Charles if she could help it.

"I'll accept your apology, David, but I will warn you, I have a way to annoy people," she warned. "Oliver would just laugh from my sarcasm or snide remarks."

His eyes looked down at her stomach. Without thinking, her hand was resting on her stomach.

"Did I hurt you when I was on top of you?" he asked.

"No. I'm sturdy, and it's going to take a lot more than throwing me to the ground to hurt this baby or me."

"May I touch you?" he asked.

"I'm not showing much."

"I just want to feel."

Gabrielle never went along this journey with a man, so she was open to David's genuine concern and curiosity about the baby.

His voice was so gentle, reminding her so much of Oliver, and of course, Gabrielle couldn't refuse. She walked up to him with a nod and took David's hand while opening her coat. Guiding his palm to place below her belly button, she had to look up into his face to see his reaction.

David was staring at his hand as if he was going to feel something. "You can't feel it yet, right?"

"Not yet. Maybe in a couple of months."

"And you have to take off work because you're high risk, correct?"

"Yes. My doctor has said I should sit my butt down for the rest of this pregnancy."

David just stared down at his hand, and then he closed his eyes to whisper something in Hindu.

"What was that?" she asked as he withdrew his hand.

"A prayer for the baby's soul," David said. "I do understand childbirth for women is laborious and stressful to the body."

"Thank you," she said and went over to the bed to pick up the envelope with David's name. "This was in the top part of the box from Oliver with your name on it."

David came to her and looked down at the envelope sealed with his name. "I can't believe he wanted to say something to me."

She moved away, going over to the side of the bed, feeling the effects of his proximity. "Oliver was just as jealous of you as you were of him."

David looked shocked by this revelation walking towards her. "But he had it all. He could make a family, he had the business, and he was brilliant."

"I never tried to understand, Oliver. I just accepted him as he was."

"That's apparently why he loved you."

She snorted full of sarcasm, forgetting herself and sitting on the bed. "It wasn't love. It was just a comfortable friendship. One night with Oliver and it felt like an eternity had passed. He made me forget about space and time."

David sat next to her. "When we were young, I felt the same. Oliver was able to make you feel special with just a look. I envied that as well about my brother."

Looking up at David, she could almost forget everything she hated about him and drown in his eyes, but she pulled herself back, fought for control, and looked away. David wasn't Oliver.

David seemed to read her thoughts. "I must remind you so much of my brother."

"No, you're meaner," she pouted, pulling the steel case in her lap as if to protect her from him.

David chuckled. "You don't pull any punches with that mouth of yours, Ms. Payne."

"I have no reason to be nice to you, David." She stared down at the steel case as if it were more interesting than looking at him. "You haven't been the least nice to me."

"Thank you for giving me the envelope. You didn't have to."

"Oliver most likely entrusted me with this because I'm probably the only honest and considerate person he knew. Whether I like you or not, I will do as I'm asked to do."

"It must be hard to look upon me knowing I'm not like my brother. You must miss him physically a lot."

She had to look at him now because she felt he was trying to dig for information. "Oliver and I weren't regular lovers." Touching her stomach, she said, "This was a one-time deal. We used protection, but I have a feeling it wasn't enough."

David frowned. "One time with my brother, you get pregnant?"

"Well, it wasn't an immaculate conception," she countered sarcastically. "And Oliver was the only man I'd been with for a long while. I've been so consumed with work and home life, having a personal life has been little to none. When Oliver came calling, I just figured he'd scratch an itch." She frowned, returning her eyes to the box. "I'm not a sex freak, if you're wondering. I like to be with people I have a connection with. Oliver had a way of making a connection right away."

"My interpersonal skills have always been a hindrance due to my condition for most of my life."

"You're only as sick as you act."

It was his turn to sound sarcastic. "So I should just pretend I don't need a kidney?"

She looked at him again earnestly. "I've found if you can't get what you want out of life, you might as well accept the life you have."

David stood up abruptly as if jolted from a dream, and she breathed a sigh of relief he'd moved away from her. "I'll leave you alone." He went over to the safe to close the door and then looked back at her. "You could have just taken this money and the jewelry."

"I could have, but it's not the amount I needed, and I don't touch what isn't mine."

There was a knock on her door, and she went to answer. From the shadow behind the frosted glass, she could identify it was Mina.

THE TROUBLE WITH GABRIELLE

The young woman was carrying a tray with tea and some small sandwiches. "My mother said you have agreed to stay, which I'm pleased about. Since you hardly touched your food, I made you some green tea, and my mother made some small sandwiches in case you became hungry later. She said the baby needs nutrition."

Looking back in the room, Gabrielle noted David had disappeared - most likely retreating to his room. The bathroom door was closed.

"Thank you, "she said to Mina, taking the tray but not welcoming the young woman in the room. "But why would you do this?"

"What do you mean?" Mina asked.

"You and Oliver were going to marry. He comes to Detroit, spends one night with me, returns, and breaks off the engagement."

Mina nodded as if to agree with Gabrielle. "When he returned, I could tell something had changed for him. He said he broke it off because he realized he wanted to be happy and not just settled. He wished he had spoken up a long time ago like David. At the time, I didn't suspect another woman. Oliver faded into depression a lot over the years, but this time I had a feeling he wasn't going to do that anymore. I have no ill will towards you because you are carrying my stepfather's legacy. He was always worried about that, and I worried for him. I was marrying Oliver to help, but I appreciate you taking that from my hands."

Gabrielle felt the woman was honest, but Oliver didn't trust many people and had not trusted this woman with his secrets.

"Thank you again, Mina. Good night."

Mina nodded and walked across the hall.

Closing the door, Gabrielle set the tray down and smelled the tea. It was still hot, and she sipped a little. As hungry as she would be in the middle of the night, she couldn't take a bite of the sandwiches.

She almost screamed as something abruptly rubbed against her leg. Looking down, she saw a black adult cat purring at her, looking desperate for a scratch.

Reaching down to scratch the cat's head, she read at the tag. "Nancy."

Of course, there would be a cat named Nancy around Oliver. He probably thought it was funny.

Since she wasn't going to eat the small sandwich, she put it down on the ground for the cat to have a go at it.

Taking off her coat, she pulled everything from the inside and outside pockets, plus most of the items out of her purse. Most importantly, the flask, her singe journal, and her wallet with an emergency fifty dollars inside. She'd already removed her charge cord and phone.

Hanging her coat on the hooks by the door, Gabrielle saw the cat was gone, and the sandwich was also. Placing the tray on the table by the door, she locked her bedroom door and then went back to the bed.

She put the flask and the journal inside the steel box and then pushed the box under the bed. At least until she figured out the second lock inside of the steel box, she would have somewhere safe to keep her items.

Looking through the dressers, she found some boxers and an oversized t-shirt with FW Delivers. This was likely a company shirt since she knew Oliver's last name was Farnworth, and the family business was delivering fresh Michigan farmed food to restaurants and hotels.

Her hand hit the socks in the back of the drawer, and she felt paper inside of a rolled-up sock. Smiling knowingly, Charles often did this as well.

Opening up the sock, she revealed a piece of folded-up printed paper from a google search on Aconitum Napellus. She sent a picture of the article to her son. Charles was good at research and would let her know more about anything she sent.

There was also a key to another lock. More secrets. It was late, and Gabrielle needed to sleep.

Going into the bathroom, she made double sure she locked the other door. On the counter was a guest kit with her name written on top.

There was a toothbrush, washcloth, and soap inside.

How considerate they were, she noted, but still suspicious of this whole family. From finding out Oliver was going to marry Mina. Yet, seeing how David felt comfortable putting a hand on Mina's shoulder to Neema initially hating Gabrielle's guts to being nice at the end of the night, a lot was going on.

Looking into the large mirror over the sink, she stared at herself for the longest time. Her wide dark brown eyes stared back at her with her long lashes gracing her eyelids. As she peeled the clothes from her body, she loved how her body's skin tone was flawless. The only remnants of her initial pregnancy were three silver lines on the right side of her curved waist.

At size fourteen, she had never been ashamed of her size because she remained healthy and ate as nutritious as she could. The only thing she'd ever gotten sick from was pregnancy, and each time seemed worse.

Exhaustion was overwhelming her more than all the thoughts flying through her brain, and she jumped in the shower and then got ready for bed. She unlocked David's bathroom door before she left and then closed her side, wishing she could jam something in there to keep him from coming into her room.

Making sure her phone was charged entirely before laying down, Gabrielle slipped under the covers and then let out a very long sigh.

The bed was deliciously comfortable, and after three breaths, she was asleep.

Chapter 8

Who Murdered Nancy?

At four in the morning, like clockwork, Gabrielle was rushing to the bathroom, and as quietly as possible, she emptied the little left in there. She mastered throwing up not to alert Charles, so she knew David most likely wasn't bothered either, albeit brother was closer.

Because she had not eaten as much, there wasn't much to let go of, and she was glad she had put some crackers in her coat she could force herself to eat.

Just as she was done washing her face and brushing her teeth, the door to David's side opened sharply, and he looked peeved to have his sleep disturbed, but this didn't faze her. She wasn't going to be apologetic about the side effects of her condition.

David's dark hair was ruffled, and he looked even sexier untamed. He was only wearing dark blue silk pajama bottoms but had the decency to put on a matching robe.

Annoyed he was bothering her when she wasn't trying to make her symptoms known to him, she asked sarcastically. "You aren't coming in here concerned about me, are you? Especially since you didn't initially believe I was pregnant anyway, and I know you still suspect I'm pulling your leg about this being Oliver's baby."

He flushed a little. "As I said, with so many paternity suits Oliver was constantly fighting off, there is little reason to believe you aren't one of them, but you know a lot about Oliver, which meant he shared time with you that I haven't known from any other woman." His murky gray eyes roamed down her body to her stomach. "I will admit I find pregnancy fascinating, Ms. Payne."

Gabrielle spilled out rudely, "You think your interest is because you'll never have children of your own unless you adopt."

He stiffened considerably.

She was going to apologize, but she started to feel nauseated again and braced herself on the counter because the room had begun to pulse along with her stomach.

David reached into the medicine cabinet, opened a bottle of peppermint, and put it under her nose. Within a minute, Gabrielle was feeling a lot better.

"How'd you learn that trick?" she asked, fascinated.

"I studied with a monk overseas to help me with my pain. When I first arrived, I was still sick from the medicine I was given in America. I needed to wean myself, and I was throwing up a lot from withdrawal or feeling nauseated most of the time," he explained.

"Now that you have returned, will you go back on the medicine here?"

He shook his head. "I will continue to practice and eat what I was taught over there. It's made the pain bearable, I'm stronger, and my condition has leveled off where I can lead a comfortable lifestyle. I'm still in need, but at least I can address my brother's death, deal with everything here before I need to address my health."

Gabrielle was so grateful for his help she leaned over and kissed his cheek. "Thank you, David. This helped."

David leaned slightly closer, staring down at her.

Her body reacted, and she wasn't sure if it was responding to the way Oliver made her feel or she really could see something from the intensity in David's eyes. "I should get some more sleep before it's time to go."

"Will you consider the visitation, Ms. Payne?"

"Please call me Gabrielle, David," She corrected him before answering. "And yes, I will think about it. Don't rush me, please. Learning everything tonight has been a lot and very stressful."

He nodded respectfully, and without another word, David left her, closing his door behind him.

Gabrielle stared at the door for a moment as her thoughts envisioned him walking to his bed, pulling off that robe, revealing the nice body she already knew what it felt like to lay on top of her.

'STOP IT, GURL!' she reprimanded herself, taking a deep whiff of the peppermint before closing the bottle and leaving it on the counter in case she needed it again later.

Getting back to her bed, she ate a couple of the crackers wrapped in an old paper towel and a little bit of water she'd gotten from a bottle that had been in the personal bedroom refrigerator. She looked at the tray with the tea and sandwiches. The tea had been sitting out and was unappealing. Since the cat had nibbled on the sandwich, Gabrielle wasn't going to try that at all.

Brushing her teeth again, she got back in bed but happened to look at the frosted glass door and was sure she saw a shadow of someone standing out there.

It was too dark to see, and her eyes could've been playing tricks on her, but she wasn't going to investigate.

Instead, Gabrielle forced herself to return to sleep, still afraid to move because she knew she'd be rushing back to the bathroom again.

Morning sickness sucked.

***

A loud, long scream yanked her out of her sleep, and Gabrielle sat straight up in bed. Looking around the bedroom in panic, Gabrielle remembered where she was. Jumping out of bed, she went to the door, but it felt jammed. It took several tries to open the door to the bedroom, and she was able to follow the screams, which now joined with cries and lots of talk in another language.

She returned to the dining room where she thought the voices were coming from, but there was no one in there. Instead, she followed the sounds to the back of the house where the sizeable kitchen was situated, and in the far corner, Neema was hysterically crying in Mina's arms.

Coming around the counter in the middle of the kitchen, Gabrielle stopped dead in her tracks to see the cat from last night laid on the floor, eyes wide open and tongue hanging out.

Grabbing the towel from the counter, she laid it over the dead cat.

Mina thanked her with a nod. This seemed to calm Neema down a little, and Mina could escort her mother out of the room.

Gabrielle knelt and pulled the towel away. The cat couldn't have been more than ten years old and seemed well taken care of from what she remembered last night.

The way the eyes bulged out and the mouth was stretched open; the cat didn't look as if it died peacefully or from old age. The look of pain seemed clear on the cat's face. Raising the cat's head slightly, Gabrielle saw it had spit up a little before dying, and its body covered the vile.

Moving the cat's body off the throw-up, she noticed the bits of sandwich she had given the cat last night. The same sandwich Mina said Neema had made.

Returning the cat to the spot, Gabrielle threw the towel back over the body and stood up as Mina returned to the kitchen.

"Thank you so much," the young woman said. "I couldn't move her or calm her down."

"Her cat must've meant a lot to her," Gabrielle sympathized.

Mina shook her head. "It was Oliver's cat. Nancy was getting up there in age, and since Oliver's passing, she's been rather stoic. Maybe seeing you in his room was her way of giving up, knowing he would never come back."

"I'm so sorry."

"It's not your fault. You didn't kill the cat, Ms. Payne. Such is life." Mina sighed and started to make tea at the Keurig. "David is coming down to remove the cat."

Seconds later, David appeared half-dressed. He only wore a tank top and dress pants. Coming around the kitchen's island, he grimaced at the sight, picked up the cat, and left out of the back glass doors of the house.

"Could you take this tea to my mother in the family room at the front of the house, Ms. Payne?" Mina asked.

As much as she didn't want to, Gabrielle still took the tray and walked down the hall. Mostly because she didn't want to stare stupidly at David when he returned in that sexy ass tank top and his usual swagger, she found herself increasingly aroused by.

Oliver had to work with words to bring the arousal out of her, while David pulled it without even trying.

Neema was wiping her eyes and trying to compose herself when Gabrielle walked in.

"Thank you," the older woman said kindly. "I didn't mean to lose it, but finally burying Oliver and now losing his cat... it was just too much."

Out of curiosity, Gabrielle questioned, "Why did you wait so long to bury him?"

"We'd already cremated him. We were waiting for David to put his affairs in order overseas so he could come back and run the business. Mina and I know nothing about running a delivery company, and since David worked there as a young man, we asked if he could come back and help us. He had been living in Indonesia for ten years since... well, since being on the oust with his father, and had to sell his house over there and get his personal life together to move back to the states."

Neema tried to dry her eyes with the wet tissue. Gabrielle quickly went across the room and retrieved some fresh tissue for the woman thinking the entire endeavor of closing one life and moving across the world would be a lot. Still, the opportunity to run his family's business must've meant a lot to David.

Neema stood and wandered to the glass balcony windows. "You do what you have to do for your child's happiness, but sooner or later, you have to be happy too."

Gabrielle wasn't sure what that meant.

"I never thought I would see a grandchild," Neema continued. "I never thought I would hear little feet around this home."

Gabrielle moved her arms around her stomach protectively. "I still haven't decided about giving anyone any visitation to my child."

"You ask us for money without the benefit of anything, Ms. Payne?"

"I've done everything on my own, ma'am. I planned on raising my child without any involvement."

"Can we compromise if I show you something?"

Gabrielle couldn't forget her original goal of getting some money to help her through this rough patch. Sharing her child with these people, Oliver never said a kind word about it would be difficult.

"I don't think you can show me anything that would change my mind," Gabrielle responded determinedly.

Neema came to Gabrielle. "Please, follow me," she insisted and proceeded to walk out of the room.

Reluctantly, Gabrielle followed, reminding herself this woman had prepared the sandwiches last night, which were intended for her. Sandwiches she partially still had in her room and wondered if she could get it analyzed.

They returned to the second floor just like last night, but this time walked past all the side rooms until they came to the end of the hall bedroom doors.

Neema took a deep breath as if to brace herself for something horrible, and even Gabrielle stiffened up a little as the older woman pushed open the double doors. "I never thought I could ever step in this room, but when Oliver agreed to marry Mina, I knew that was a chance at something new to push the old memories away. A grandchild would be a reset. A way to start everything over again where this could be home and not just a house. A way I could come into this room."

Gabrielle looked down at the doorway and noticed how Neema didn't cross the threshold. "Sadness is keeping you back?"

"A life loss. My Joseph died here, wishing he had a legacy to leave." The older woman touched her heart. "I know things cannot be the same unless his dying wish is fulfilled." She looked at Gabrielle. "If you've been sent to help my Joseph fulfill that wish, then I will do anything for you in your time of need, but please, do not deny me the pleasure of a grandchild."

Sarcastically, Gabrielle wanted to point out this would be the woman's step-grandchild, but she pursed her lips together to stop things from falling from her mouth.

Neema further offered, "We can stay close to Detroit, where the company has rental property. There are two apartments there we can move into until the birth. And not only would we give you the amount needed, but we'll cover any medical cost."

There was an honest look of desperation on her face.

Neema continued. "I'm not looking for any custody, but just like David, family means a lot to me, and you carry our family, Ms. Payne. I want to make sure the life of the child has the best opportunity possible."

Gabrielle still didn't trust this woman to file some changes to take custody of the unborn baby or, for that matter, once they found out about Charles to do more to hurt her. If she agreed to make their family whole, it could destroy the little family she had.

"I'll arrange to take you down to Detroit to look at the apartments today, get some clothes to come back up and join us for dinner and stay one more night. If your place of stay isn't suitable, we can even arrange for you to move to the apartments," Neema suggested. "Tomorrow, whatever you agree to, I will still write out a check for whatever amount you want. I promise. I want you to give us a chance."

Getting back to Detroit and checking on Charles would be perfect! Yet, she would still have to return to this place tonight.

Looking at the bedroom now turned into a large nursery and play area; she could envision Charles here having fun in the corner while the baby slept snuggled in the bed. Neema, despite her initial cruelty, would probably dote on the children to the point of spoiling, yet still be nurturing, unlike Gabrielle's mother.

That gnawing feeling that someone tried to poison her last night still irked her, but why would Neema be the culprit if now she offered all of this?

Gabrielle was perplexed.

'Keep your eyes on the goal. Do whatever you have to do to get the money for now and then go from there.'

"I'll go look at the apartments and then get some clothes to come back for dinner, but I'll still think about staying tonight. Honestly, Neema, I don't think I can stand... another night away from home." She almost said, 'being around you people,' but changed her words at the last minute.

Neema clapped her hands excitedly. "I'll have David arrange for the car immediately."

Gabrielle returned to her bedroom and was glad to see the plate was still on the table by the door, where she left it with the remnants of the sandwich. She grabbed some tissue and wrapped a little bit of the sandwich up.

Mina appeared at the door suddenly. "I can take that tray down."

"Thank you," Gabrielle said.

"You didn't eat much?"

"I wasn't feeling well. If I don't eat before a certain time, I'll get ill."

"Like you were this morning?" Mina replied.

How this woman knew Gabrielle was praying to the porcelain God's this morning was uncomfortable to note. So Mina had been a figure at the frosted panes?

In a dismissive tone, Gabrielle said, "Please let your mother know I'll be down in a moment."

Mina left, and Gabrielle closed the door and put on her coat. She stuffed the piece of sandwich in her inside pocket, picked up the steel case, put her charge card in her coat pocket, and was ready to leave.

Gabrielle called her son, knowing he was in school, and planned on leaving a message, but Charles answered.

"Hello there, mother," he said as if he expected her call. "Are you okay?"

"No and yes. There is something strange going on. I found a paper on something in my friend's dresser. Did you get my text about it?"

"Yes, that's a poison called Monkshood," he answered authoritatively. "We're studying plants in biology. I did a paper on poison plants found in Michigan, and that's the most dangerous. It's a purple flower - really pretty." He spoke as if reciting from a book, but she knew most likely Charles had remembered the text by heart. "No cure if ingested, and it can cause heart arrhythmia."

"And most likely, no one would be looking for it if there had been an autopsy," Gabrielle surmised.

"Most likely," her son agreed. "You think someone gave it to him, Momma?"

"I got some sandwiches last night, and I didn't eat them. I let the cat have them, and this morning they found the cat dead."

"Do you have any of the sandwiches?" Charles asked.

"Yes, but how would I be able to prove my friend ingested them?"

There was silence on the other line, and she could almost hear Charles thinking.

"If it was fed to the friend intermittently, there could be proof in the hair follicles. Can you get those? Or have they cleaned up after him?"

She looked around the room and then went into the bathroom. On her side of the bed was a drawer with an O carved meticulously on there, while on the other side by David's door, there was an old English D carved on that drawer.

She opened Oliver's drawer to see there were used hair and teeth brushing items. "I have his hairbrush, comb, and toothbrush."

Charles called someone to him. "Would you be able to use the lab to look at something for me?"

"Sure, Charles. Anything for you," a woman's voice said.

"Who is that?" Gabrielle asked protectively, shoving the majority of the drawer in the inner pocket of her jacket.

"It's a friend, Zuri Carter, who studied Forensic Science. She was my lab partner and really smart when it comes to Forensics, Momma," he answered without worrying about her. "I can't believe she walked by just as we were having this conversation. Can I get those items soon? "

"I'm coming back today to grab some things and return here, but I'll drop off the sandwich and the items at home." She packed her purse quickly.

With his voice filled with concern, Charles asked, "Are you going to be okay, Momma?"

"Yes," she assured him.

"Don't eat the food," he warned.

"I won't."

"Or drink anything."

"Yes, love."

"I love you," he said.

She wanted to cry at how doting her son was.

"I love you too, Charles," she said. "Bye, my love." She hung up the phone.

The door to David's bathroom door opened, and the man didn't look too happy, but the fact he was still wearing that tank top, and his pants were wide open was what drew her eyes.

Darkly tanned skin, matted with dark curly hair all over his chest, making a pathway down a rippled stomach to disappear in briefs. Gabrielle couldn't stop looking, and she prayed she didn't drool. Oliver shaved his chest and kept his face clean-shaven, while David had this wild man, almost savage look when he wasn't fully dressed.

'Lawd, help her senses,' she prayed to herself as she forced her eyes away from him.

"Who's Charles? Your tone of voice was deceptively loving and nurturing to a college-bound son," David demanded to know.

Chapter 9

Not Your Average Ten-Year-Old

Gabrielle knew her son was different when he was three months and pointed at sight cards correctly. When Charles was six months, he picked up the book his mother read to him every night and started reading in his baby talk.

By eight months, he could form sentences and

His affinity to plants and animals came when she lived in a two-family flat. The downstairs neighbor who often babysat Charles worked in the backyard garden and owned four dogs, six cats, two hamsters, four rabbits, three turtles, a lizard, and two different kinds of snakes.

Charles started talking in complete sentences by one. To help him accelerate, the babysitters she hired were also teachers and privately kept up his accelerated study. Of course, this costs her an arm and a leg, but it was very much worth it when he graduated by nine from high school with an Associates in Veterinary Technician, with a minor in Botany.

As her son progressed in life, she knew he was extraordinary, but she also treated him like a child. She was fostering him to play outside instead of always being holed up in his room studying and taking him on camping trips and biking weekends, even if it was to sleep in their car since she couldn't afford a trailer.

As much as Gabrielle doted on her son, Charles doted on her and showed how much he cared for her all the time.

Now with David standing there in the doorway, the upper half of him fully naked, looking like Michelangelo used his body for the now-famous statue, she slowly turned around, tearing her eyes from the visual deliciousness. Catching her breath, trying to contain her sexual excitement, and said, "He's my son. I told you about him. W-Why are you listening to my conversation?"

He looked embarrassed. "I didn't mean to listen to your conversation, Ms... Gabrielle. I came up to change my clothes so we could leave and I heard you speaking on the phone. You were talking intimately, and it just didn't seem you were talking to a college-bound young man," David said. "I'm sorry for eavesdropping."

She shook her head, needing to get the subject off of Charles. "It's fine. You have every reason to believe this baby isn't Oliver's, but it is, and as soon as you give me my money, I'll be out of your hair."

"Not according to Neema," David retorted. "She's convinced you to see the apartments in Detroit so she can stay closer to the child? I'd hate to get her hopes up high and then find out you're lying."

"Well, I'm not, and I told her I would consider everything. I've said nothing to hold me in a court of law." She could still see he hadn't put on a shirt yet from her peripheral vision. "Could you please put on some clothes!" she exclaimed.

He walked away from the bathroom doorway, and she breathed a sigh of relief, composing herself. After quickly standing up and grabbing the steel case, Gabrielle went to the front door where Neema was waiting.

"Is the car here yet?" she questioned.

"Oh, David said he can take you. He left some items in the apartments when he initially flew in, and he needs to pick them up."

Gabrielle's stomach did a quadruple backflip. "I-I don't know-"

Neema cut her off pleadingly. "He's promised to be on his best behavior. He'll take you wherever you want to go, and it's just my assurance you will return tonight."

Cutting her eyes, she asked, "Whether I want to or not?"

"We're not forcing you, Ms. Payne," Neema said coolly. "We do want to be a part of the baby's life."

David joined them in the hall. From the side of her eye, she could see he had changed into a t-shirt and some jeans with a fall jacket. Just swagalicious! Dammit.

"The car is in the garage," David said. "We can go through the back of the house."

Gabrielle took the initiative and opened the door to get some distance from him. "I'll wait out here for you."

New air to breathe and a moment of peace away from everything gave her renewed purpose. Whether it was her pregnancy hormones or just her attraction to David's constant reminder of what she dreamed Oliver looked like, Gabrielle's body was coming and going constantly.

He pulled up in a silver new four-door Honda and came around to open the door for her to get in on the passenger side.

Gabrielle clearly showed him a disdain for his gentlemanly ways as she sat down in the car and watched him intently get on the other side. Would Oliver have done the same? She wondered. Since she'd never gone out with Oliver, she would never know the answer to that question.

David drove away from the house, nervously cleared his throat, and then asked, "I didn't want to ask this around Neema and Mina, but what kind of things did Oliver pay you to do? Did you do something special sexually for Oliver that he couldn't get from all the other women he frivolously slept around with?"

Gabrielle cut him an even more complex look, but hopefully, telling the truth about Oliver would make him dislike her and cause her not to be so damn attracted to David. "As I said, Oliver liked to talk with me. He liked that I was honest with him all the time and could see through the facade he showed everyone else."

He shifted in his seat and asked, "When was the last doctor's appointment for the baby?"

"I've only had one, and that was a week ago. I can give you the doctor's name and sign any release form you wish if that's going to prevent you from giving me my money. I'm not afraid of you, David, and I'm not lying."

"I haven't called you a liar."

"You are a man who believes action speaks louder than words, and you feel the truth is just going to come out somehow. I'm telling the truth." She changed the subject and asked, "Did you read your letter?"

David glanced at her, annoyed. "Was there anything else in the box for me?"

"There was another lock, but also a letter for me, but I didn't read it because I wanted to be away from your family before I did." In honesty, she wanted to be close to Charles if she needed to share something or was scared the letter might make her feel so sad she needed her son nearby for comfort.

Pulling the steel case on her lap, she opened the box to show another smaller safe inside. "I can't figure this combination out, but I know Oliver left it for me. If the will is in there, I will return it to the family."

Confidently, David said, "The will is not in there. That box is just for you. Oliver told me this in my letter."

Gabrielle felt they'd come to a silent agreement to put up with each other. He kept the car at a decent speed - not too fast and not too slow.

The silence between them didn't bother her, but she was deeply curious about David and his life that Oliver couldn't have told her.

"What did you do in Indonesia away from your family, and why did he go so far?

"Healing on another level, and I went to discover my mother's family," he answered as if he was relieved someone asked. "My mother's father had gotten another woman pregnant even though he was pledged to marry another. He took the woman he loved, eloped to the United States, and started the delivery company. By the time my father and mother married, the business was failing, but my father promised to make the business a success if my grandfather sold him everything. My father changed the name and did what he promised to do. And then he taught us how to keep it a success."

She realized out loud, "You went there to find out if there was some other stipulation somewhere you could get the company back or anything your grandfather's parents had left him you could claim, didn't you, David?"

"My grandfather's family was happy to see me, but the only thing they wanted from me was to help them keep my grandfather's promise and marry into the family he had broken the pledge. They felt they were cursed and shamed because of what my grandfather did. I couldn't help them because of my health, and I could not marry someone I did not have feelings for. It was why I was broken from my family in the first place."

"Were you jealous Oliver received your birthright?"

He shook his head. "Oliver had been very successful at keeping the company making profits despite the competition and economy. I've been away for so long, and honestly, I know nothing about running the business now, but I will do my best and make my grandparents proud. I can't be mad at Oliver. I believe if I had been given the company, my health would have suffered. I had to leave the country for medical reasons. I was desperate for treatment to slow down my condition, which couldn't be found in the US. There were studies in Europe and China that had been successful. Being on the other continent was better for my research and health. Now that I've returned, hopefully, a donor would be found since I am in peak physical condition and would be able to endure surgery."

All she could do was repeat "peak physical condition" in her brain repeatedly while she visually thought about him with no top on and what that path of hair leading into his pants.

He would look at her occasionally with a frown, and she knew he was trying to see what she was thinking, but she wouldn't give him eye contact. She was deathly afraid of what would fall out of her mouth.

They arrive at the apartments close to the New Center area in the middle of The City of Detroit. Surprisingly, it was right down the street from the hospital where Gabrielle had chosen to have the baby. The side-by-side housing created great condo living right outside a high-end gated community. The family owned about twenty units and was buying a massive lot from the city to build twenty more, a community garden and play area, plus a private recreation center for their inhabitants.

They were facing east, so she had to use her hand to cover her eyes to look over the vacant lot next to the property. "Looks like you've been thinking of this for a very long time," she noted.

"I've always wanted to come home, but until my father died, there wasn't any reason. I helped others run their properties while away, and I think I can make a great deal of income on the backend for our family, given a chance. Neema is going to give me that chance," he said.

"But only if you marry her daughter," she pointed out.

"I'm willing to do whatever I have to do to bring my family business back to where it belongs," he said fiercely.

She only shrugged, not wishing to go into what was morally wrong, but who was she to judge when she admitted she had taken money for sex. Right now, David believed she was still a prostitute.

"Are you in pain?" David asked abruptly.

"No," she answered. "Why?"

"You touch your stomach a lot."

"Eating is hard," she admitted. "I just barely had any dinner yesterday and since then, more or less, just tea from Mina."

"Can you eat now?"

"Just a little. Late morning is usually the only good time."

He was still looking at her stomach like he had been looking this morning with a yearning. "Does it bother you? My pregnancy?" she asked.

"No," he said apologetically. "Like I said this morning, it's just fascinating."

She smiled. "It's too small to feel anything."

"I know. I'm sorry if I make you feel uncomfortable." He walked her back to the car.

David left her a moment to go inside one of the condos to retrieve some items, and when he returned to the vehicle, Gabrielle gave him instructions to her home.

"You don't make me feel uncomfortable," she said, continuing the conversation. "I think it's rather odd. You and Oliver seem so different. He was far from the fatherly type, yet you seem to want to be there every waking moment."

"Perhaps because he could procreate, and he took that for granted, and I cannot. I want to appreciate the journey. Despite being on the outs with my father, I still admire that he was a very strong and wonderful dad, and I dream of raising a child from my bloodline to take over my family's business, and know a little of my culture, morals, and values."

She almost wished David had been there for Charles.

"Did I say something wrong?" David asked uncomfortably.

"Why are you trying to be so nice to me, David? Because Neema will be upset with you if I don't want to come back?"

"Honestly, that is one reason, and the other is if you are carrying Oliver's child, I would hate to spoil my chance to be a part of the child's life."

"So, you need me to like you?"

"I think we should be cordial."

To torture his kindness, Gabrielle questioned, "What are you willing to do to make me like you?"

The car jerked a little as he shifted uncomfortably.

"I'm just kidding," she said quickly. "I didn't mean to make you drive off the road."

He cleared his throat. "I didn't...."

Gabrielle chuckled at his sudden uncomfortableness.

"I mean, I read that pregnant women do have heightened hormones and desire to have sex more," he pointed out.

She didn't recall if this happened in her first pregnancy, but being around David, she found hormones going everywhere. It was her turn to shift uncomfortably. "Well, of course, I wouldn't put that responsibility on you when I know you can't."

"A man's member is not the only way to please a woman," he countered and then blushed at his forwardness.

Impressed, Gabrielle said mockingly, trying to make light of the sexually explicit subject, "Well, look who took a class on how to please a woman?"

He stopped in front of her address and said, "If you cannot have sex to procreate, you come to a better understanding of the power of sex to the human soul."

She pretended to slowly look away from him and gripped the handle of the door tight. Did David's words just make her come?

THE TROUBLE WITH GABRIELLE

Chapter 10

Possibly Blowing This Out of Proportion

Charles was waiting in the foyer and rushed in her arms as soon as she entered the house, closing the door as she came into the home. Gabrielle almost dropped the steel box she held from his muscular frame. Although he only came to her chest and looked lean, he had always been a heavy child of pure brawn.

"Are you okay?" Gabrielle asked, worried.

He looked up at her, his murky grey and tannish eyes beamed in concern. "I should be asking you," he said, pushing a black cowlick from his face. Her son had opted to keep his hair long, always groaning when she even mentioned trimming his hair. "I didn't expect you home as soon as I got home."

"I got a ride. The car... It's broken." She couldn't tell her son how stupid she had been to blow up their car.

He released his death grip around her waist and looked out the window at the car she had gotten out of. "Why is the driver still out there?"

"Because I'm going back to find out what happened to my friend," she said.

Her son looked at her suspiciously. "You can't go back there. Where's the paper you said you found about the flower?"

She opened the steel box where she had kept the paper and handed it to her son.

Retrieving his backpack, he took out some paper and showed it to her. "I don't know who these people are, but if someone is looking up Monkshood, other than to grow it, they were suspicious about its poisonous properties. How did this friend die?"

"A heart attack."

He shuffled through one of his papers and said, "The poison could cause elevated heart rates and breathing fluctuations."

Shaking her head, Gabrielle disputed, "But this is his family."

"We both know family still can hurt each other," Charles said with sarcasm.

Her mother came to the doorway. "You didn't drop enough money in my account," her mother complained.

"Speak of the devil," her son snipped.

Giving Charles a sharp mute look, Gabrielle addressed her mother, "And how much more did you need, Ingrid?"

"How long are you thinking of making me stay here?" her mother asked.

"One more day."

Ingrid crinkled her already dark, wrinkled face shuffling her false teeth in her mouth as if deep in thought. "Then I'm going to need twice the amount I asked for, Gab."

That would drain Gabrielle's account, and she had no one else to call to watch Charles unless she took him with her.

"I don't need a babysitter," Charles protested.

Her son was right, but the last thing Gabrielle needed was someone calling the cops because they saw a little boy coming and going from the house without parental supervision.

Stiffly, Gabrielle agreed, "I can send the money to your account tonight, Mom."

"Well, hurry it up." Her mother left the room.

"She's not a good influence on me," Charles said.

Rolling her eyes, she said, "I have to go back, Charles."

"Did you at least bring the sandwich or anything?"

Gabrielle handed him the sample of the sandwich stuffed down in her jacket's pocket, and then she went to her room. With her Ranch style two-bedroom rental, it wasn't much, but it was what she could afford. With the baby coming, she would have to look for another place to stay, but that was another adult problem she would not stress her son with.

Before putting the steel case under her bed, Gabrielle took out the letter and made sure she put it in her coat. Oliver's unread letter could hold the secret to the second lock. Her heart was not ready to bury him away, and she knew reading the letter was most likely his goodbye to her.

After changing into a lovely yellow top and gray yoga pants with a boot flare, she grabbed her overnight bag. Adding only some clothes and a makeup case for just tomorrow, she promised herself to return and not look for anything that wasn't there.

And you'll resist David Farnsworth!

When she came down, Charles was standing at the window staring down at David's car as if he was trying to blow up the vehicle with his eyes. She saw the stoical stance with his arms crossed over his body.

"I'm going to be okay," she assured her son.

Charles didn't look back at her.

"I won't eat anything," she promised.

He reached out his arm with a thick paper bag. "Take this."

She took the bag and looked inside. There were crackers, some peanut butter and jelly sandwiches, cookies, and water.

"Not a drop of food," he said sharply.

Kissing her son's brow, she said, "Not a crumb from the house," she swore.

He nodded and gave her the death grip hug again. "I love you, momma."

Closing her eyes and relishing the moment, knowing her son was getting too old for the sappiness, Gabrielle said tenderly. "And I love you too, Charles. Take care of Grandma, and I'll see you tomorrow."

Her son intently watched her walk out the door, and she could feel him return to the window and knew he was watching her.

David jumped out of the car as she came to him. "You don't have the steel box," he noted.

"I left it," she said. "I know I'll be back for it."

"Of course," he said with disappointment, but then paused for a moment and looked at her home, right where she knew Charles was staring, but she knew David couldn't see the boy.

"Is everything okay," she questioned.

"It's weird," he answered. "I feel like Oliver is somewhere near."

Trying to laugh it off, she teased, "If he were, I think we should hurry up and get in the car."

David put her bag in the back and then opened the car door for her.

Gabrielle didn't relax until they were a block away. "So tell me all about this healing across the ocean you received," she said, trying to get his mind off of whatever he was thinking.

"As I said, it was needed," he responded. "When I couldn't reconcile with my father, and it didn't look like I would be placed on any donor list too soon, I used what money I had to find some peace."

"And that's where the monks came in?" she questioned, just glad to be off the Oliver subject.

Perhaps because they were twins, Charles' presence could be felt by David through his father's genes. Gabrielle didn't want to try to understand, but it would be best to keep her son away from this family until she could be sure they couldn't take him away or cause any harm to her.

"Yes," David answered. "I've completely gotten myself from so much medicine, and I'm trying to make sure I stay as healthy as possible."

David turned into a restaurant where a long line awaited outside, but they drove around to the rear, where he assisted her from the car.

"Can I ask you something personal?" she asked, looking up into his gray-brown eyes.

"Anything," he said with a deep passion that gave her goosebumps and almost made her forget what she wanted to ask.

"How long can you survive... like you are?"

"I don't know, but I want to live every day as if it counts, and I'm willing to put right what was torn apart." He looked down at her stomach. "I have to tell you a secret, Gabrielle."

As hard as it was to look into his eyes, she continued to do so and waited.

"I read my brother's letter. He said your name in the letter. He told me to take care of the Angel's Heart."

Unconsciously, she touched her stomach, but she had a feeling Oliver was speaking of Charles. Oliver couldn't have been sure about the baby so soon. Had Oliver revealed Charles in his letter to David? It took everything inside of her not to look panicked.

"Without a doubt, Oliver's letter has solidified that you are the mother to his child. And if you need anything from me-"

Cutting him off suspiciously, Gabrielle asked, "Are you nice to me because you want the business?"

"I would do anything for Oliver."

"Even though he took your legacy and stood on his father's side?"

He looked a little bitter for a second but then responded, "As much as I knew he hated it, if Oliver had not taken over the company, Neema would have gotten the company. It was my mother's company. My grandparents worked hard, and I don't think they would have wanted it to be owned by anyone other than their bloodline. Family meant everything to my grandparents, but love meant more. I loved that business. I love what my family has created." He pressed his hand over hers that was on her stomach. "And I'll love my brother's child as if he were my own."

Having his proximity and touch simultaneously was a bit overwhelming, but she forced herself to keep everything together. "He?" Gabrielle snorted, using sarcasm as a defense to her arousal. "We aren't sure what the gender of the child is."

"You're right." David moved his hand away. "I shouldn't have assumed or pressed my machinations on you."

"Is that the only secret?" she questioned. "From the letter? Is there something else I should know?"

"Nothing at this time. Are you able to eat?" he questioned.

She was famished and grateful for someone else thinking of her needs, but she took note he seemed to change the subject away from the letter. "I'd love to," she said.

David guided her into an employee entrance, and an employee seemed to recognize him immediately and pointed them up the stairs. The carpeted flight of stairs led to a long low lit hallway, and David opened the door to a room on the left just past a set of bathrooms. This room seemed too large for just two people. There a blue decor around the room, and artificial candles lit the area. Extra chairs and tables neatly lined the room, but there was a semi-large circular table enough for six people to sit around in the middle, but only two chairs were there.

A dinner setting was placed, and David pulled out a chair for her.

His gentlemanly ways were starting to get to her too, and she needed a distraction before she found herself adoring him too much.

"May I go to the bathroom?" she asked.

"Yes." He pointed her in the direction of the bathroom, which was just off the stairs down a hallway.

Gabrielle left the room and proceeded to freshen up, telling herself repeatedly this was getting something to eat.

Oliver had never taken her out on any date, and she was having two babies by that man, but his brother... Was he courting her? Or was he being nice to get his hands on her baby to control his family's business?

When would they try to prove she was an unfit mother?

Or would something worse happen?

There was this sudden flush overwhelming her body and it took a moment to gather her equilibrium. All of this she blamed on David and his proximity doing a number on all her senses.

Keep your focus, Gabrielle. She encouraged herself. Oliver said these people made him miserable, and Gabrielle needed to stay on her toes because all this nicety could be a way to get her to let her guard down.

When she returned, David stood to help her off with her jacket, and she watched as he hung it by the door. She didn't trust anyone with her coat because of everything it

contained. It was like her purse with all its many pockets...
including Oliver's letter and her wallet.

"I find it strange you never asked about our names," David said.

"Why? Oliver told me freely. He was quite talkative. Said your grandmother loved Charles Dickens. Your mother was named after Charles Dickens' oldest daughter. You even named your first dog Dickens, right?"

David looked surprised. "Oliver spoke that deep of me?"

"Not a lot. No dark secrets because he said you only tried to be honest with yourself and be damn everyone else, including family."

His look was filled with guilt. "Oliver didn't understand. He was healthy all his life. Every time my father saw me, I knew he was upset at me, even when I was young. My father felt I was weak and would not carry on the business," David said. "He used my love for another woman as a way to push me away."

"Money isn't everything,' she said disdainfully.

"Really? Because I thought that was why you revealed yourself to us."

"Paying bills is important. Not being hungry is important. Trying to make a better life for my family is important, but even if Neema doesn't give me the money, I would still find another way to support my family. It would be tough as hell, but just like you, I'm willing to do anything." This was a dig to bite at his conscience.

"It's not the money, Gabrielle. It's the business for me. Yes, it affords us a nice lifestyle and helps us to acquire assets, but it would all mean nothing if the family is not there to share the riches from the hard work." David twirled a ring on his right pinky, and Gabrielle remembered Oliver had a ring just like that.

Their mother had given them the quartz ring with an engraved feather polished over it. Oliver's ring was silver, and David's was gold.

"My grandparents came to America arriving in Boston, where they didn't know a lick of English. My grandmother was earning a Ph.D. and needed work. She cleaned a museum at night while my grandfather worked in the plant during the day and worked his business at night. They had books by Charles Dickens, and she would carefully read each one until she learned English on her own and then would come home and teach my father."

A woman entered the private dining room, pushing a tray to the table. She curtsied and said something in Hindu to David. He chuckled, and the woman clicked her tongue, nodded at Gabrielle, and left.

"She said you were glowing and pretty," David said. "I teased her and said I do that to people, but we know that is a lie, right?"

"Oh, most definitely," Gabrielle agreed, going along with his ribbing.

The food smelled delicious, and David pulled off the lids of soups, meats, sides, and bread.

"How were you able to get this private space?" she questioned. "Does your family own this place too?"

"No. We deliver to this restaurant. My father expanded the business to Southwestern restaurants and hotels, but with the economic downturn, it's slowed up a bit. I've tried to keep up with the business even though I've been away, and from what I gathered, Oliver was coming up with a plan, but he left little notes at the office, and I've searched his bedroom for a notebook but couldn't find anything. Oliver kept most of his thoughts to himself, so this is no surprise; that is why I'm so fascinated he revealed so much to you."

"Most times, I think he said things to shock me or make me hate him, and other times, it seemed as if he needed to get a lot off his chest."

"But no matter what he said, you never seem to hate him."

"I try to feel about a person by the way they treat me," she admitted.

"I can understand why you dislike me then."

Gabrielle stuffed a lot of food into her mouth, trying to avoid the feeling of the effects of David's words. Yet something had shifted in her soul suddenly, and this affected her whole body. At the same time, her chest started to swell, and inadvertently she touched her breast to contain the discomfort.

"Are you okay," David asked with concern. "You're suddenly sweating, Gabrielle."

If she didn't stop eating, it would feel like she had to burst, and until the swelling went down, she could barely speak. Her milk production had started early with Charles at the most inopportune time, which was no different. Holding her finger up to give herself a moment to collect herself was all Gabrielle could do.

David stared at her the whole time, first in concern and then in fascination.

Embarrassed once she could think straight, she moved her hands away from her chest. "I'm sorry. There was swelling," she explained.

"It looked uncomfortable," he said.

"It was," she agreed, finding it odd to speak to someone about her pregnancy. "I'm not used to sharing my experience."

"I take it your son's father was not around?"

"No, and he still isn't," she said. This was the first very accurate statement about Charles.

He looked bothered. "I find that terrible. I'd want to be there for every moment. I think a woman's pregnancy is just magical. Can I ask a favor of my own?"

"It depends," she said.

"May I be there? I want to go to some doctor's visits, and if you choose a natural birth, I will be honored to be chosen as a breathing partner so that I can be there in the delivery room? I don't think I'll ever have that opportunity on my own."

Just as the swelling was going down, it was starting to return.

That was a lot to ask of her. Something she'd always wished a man would ask of her and if David wanted to be so involved, maybe thinking they wanted to harm her was blowing things out of proportion.

THE TROUBLE WITH GABRIELLE

CHAPTER 11

MAY I TOUCH YOU

Gabrielle could imagine David staying beside her helping her breathe. During her clinical, she would jealousy look at the men being supportive. David would be one of those men staring deep into her eyes and being caught up in the process while whispering sweet and adoring words to her.

The look on his face caught her heart up, and she couldn't say no. "I guess it's fine, David, as long as I'm given full parental rights to my child, and you guys aren't going to take it away."

"Is that why you're hesitant about us being in the child's life?"

"Both you and Neema expressed high interest in my baby," she narrowed her eyes suspiciously. "How do I know you're not working in tangent to go to the courts behind my back to take my child away from me? Especially now that I know, it's Oliver's only living relative."

"And how do we know you aren't going to try to take what my family has built for your pleasure now that you know this information?"

She could see his side of the story. "I don't trust you, and I know you can't trust me."

David leaned back and ran a frustrated hand through his nicely cut black hair. "We agree, Gabrielle, so what do you propose we do?"

"We?" She snorted. "Unless you speak French, there is no Oui."

Sarcastically, he responded pretty fluently, "Je parle un peu français, but that's not the case."

Narrowing her eyes, shocked at his comeback, she was turned on yet again by the sexiness of his voice. "You aren't funny, David," she said, trying her best not to show her amusement. "Why should I decide this whole trust mess? Why should I make an effort to trust people that only made Oliver miserable?"

"Whether you like it or not, you hold all the cards. I want to preserve my family business, but I do want to see my nephew." He looked down at her stomach to indicate what he meant.

"We don't know the sex of the child yet," she snipped.

"Either way, I don't want to have negotiations every time I wish to spend time with Oliver's offspring, and I'm sure Neema agrees with me, which is why she is trying to show you we would welcome you and the child in however you feel comfortable,"

"And the business?"

"Once we find Oliver's will, it will most likely bequeath the majority of the business and assets to his closest blood relative. I'm hoping my brother purposely made provisions for Neema and Mina."

"And you?"

"Unfortunately, I know Oliver couldn't. He has to go with whatever my father has set up for the business legally, and I cannot interfere in that decision, but if you are the guardian of the child, you do have legal rights to choose whoever you wish to run the business."

"Which you hope I choose you?"

"False hope only gives false comfort. You do whatever has to do for the best life for your child, but I pray you make the best decision for our bloodline and family business at the same time."

She picked at her food, pondering her children's future. Charles would most likely want to be involved in some of the business, but not completely. Yet, the child she was carrying, she wasn't sure. David seemed to know a little about the company, which was why Neema asked him to come back, and this seemed like what he wanted to do.

Just as Gabrielle was about to speak again, the tightness in her chest returned, and she leaned forward to decrease the weight of her breast. The intensity this time was almost dizzying, and she put her head down to concentrate while taking deep breaths.

David came to her. Getting on his knees on the side of her, he asked, "May I touch you, Gabrielle?"

She was in too much pain to care and nodded.

Gently he raised her arms just enough for him to move his warm palm under her arm. Embarrassed that she hadn't shaved, she almost pulled away, but his pressure was insistent as he pulled her into his body so his arm could go behind her and press under her other arm. She was forced to sit up straight, and whether it was the oxytocin or just his proximity, she could feel the tightness in her breast dissipate.

Was David also magic?

When she could breathe, she said, "I think if you continue to do that, you can touch me anytime, David."

He chuckled.

Her senses went on high, and at that moment, as half her body pressed against him and his arms held her close, she could imagine being naked with David and making love like there was no tomorrow.

David said softly, "I learned that from a friend's wife. She was a doula in Indonesia. It also helps when you're trying to breastfeed, and need let down."

Moving back slightly and looking up at him, she noted, "You know a lot about a woman's pregnancy."

"Those who can't should at least be able to help or teach."

Damn, why did he have to sound so perfect? Pushing away from him, Gabrielle said, "Thank you."

He moved back to his seat. "I didn't mean to say something to make you uncomfortable."

"You didn't," she said.

The waiter returned, and David ordered something as other servers came to clean the table off.

When they were alone again, David asked, "Oliver paid to have sex with you? He ordered a prostitute, and you came?"

The question threw her off for a moment, but once recovered from David's audacity, she said with no filter, "Oliver paid for a hand job from a black woman. That's what he ordered from the service. I worked for the service specifically for that reason."

He frowned. "You often break the rules of your service."

Blushing, she said, "I never broke the rules until Oliver." Chuckling more to herself, she said, "I guess that's why he was my last customer." It felt nice to be able to speak about her life to someone.

Gabrielle would have never told Ingrid this information because she never wanted her mother to know she had resorted to becoming a sex worker after being tossed out of her home.

"What did he say to you to make you break the rules?" David asked.

Closing her eyes, she remembered clearly the first night with Oliver. "He asked me to stay with him."

"That's it?"

"I know, it sounds silly, but I guess it was more of the way he said it. He was a man torn, hurt, and ..." She couldn't think of how to describe that look in Oliver's eyes. She could only feel what he felt.

"I understand," David said quietly. "Did you mean to have unprotected sex?"

Frustrated, she said, "It was protected. I mean, Oliver did use protection. I don't go around having unprotected sex - ever. Getting pregnant just happened."

"Are you sure?" David questioned.

The waiter returned with a miniature caramel-baked dessert that smelled like heaven. Two forks accompanied the saucer.

Needing the sugar to lift her spirits from this annoying conversation with David, Gabrielle was still hungry, and she didn't hesitate to ask if they were sharing before she picked up her fork and took a piece. The baked desire just landed on her tongue and seemed to melt away into sweet goodness.

Loving the high, she took a moment to savor the food before she answered David. "Quite positive. Oliver had to get out of bed, find his pants and return while I finished taking off my heels."

"I didn't mean to say you're easy, Gabrielle," he said. "I just... Well, I think Oliver had intentions of getting you pregnant."

"How would you know?" she said. "You hadn't spoken to Oliver in forever."

"You're right, but Oliver called me some months ago. I think after he had been with you. He said he had done something that ruined someone, and there was nothing he could do to make things right on that matter, but it was the only solution to everyone's problem."

Gabrielle could feel her breathing slow. "How do you know he was speaking of me?"

He took a moment to try the dessert for himself.

Just like her, it had a powerful effect on him that he also had to close his eyes and a smile graced his lips. Damn, why did he get more handsome the more she spent time with him?

David picked up his napkin and wiped the corners of his mouth before speaking. "I didn't until I was sitting in the car outside of your home. I could almost feel Oliver had been sitting there too, talking on the phone with me."

Or his son Charles was right inside the window glaring like the devil at his uncle, she thought to herself.

"What else did Oliver say?" she persisted.

"Well, I told him he should ask for forgiveness, and He said he couldn't change what was done, but only I could make it right, and it would be exactly what I needed. He added something about making things right for everyone."

"How?"

David shrugged. "I don't know. I mean, he knew I was a world away getting the treatment I couldn't get anywhere else." He paused as if there was something wrong and looked away from her.

His expression told her he had figured something out.

"What?" she demanded.

"Nothing," he said, still not looking at her.

"David-"

"I can't," he said, now meeting her eyes.

Knowing Oliver's look when there was something that needed to be said, but he couldn't, she handled David the same way, "I don't read minds, and if you want to keep this honest-"

"I think he was trying to make things right with me and needed me to help you."

"Hence his letter?" she guessed.

"Yes."

Gabrielle felt there was more, but she didn't press him. "So taking care of me will help you?"

"There's more to it."

Despite being a drunk, Oliver was intelligent. Deceptively intelligent and there was always meaning to his madness.

Deep down in her heart, she knew Oliver had got her pregnant this second time on purpose, and David's interpretation of Oliver's plan was accurate. Yet, Oliver couldn't be sure he had conceived right after their second time.

"What are you thinking?" David questioned.

"Nothing," she lied.

He used her words against her, leaning forward. "I don't read minds, and if you-"

"I think you're right."

"What else?" he pressed.

Gabrielle felt uncomfortable in her skin again. "I think a child of Oliver's is here to help your family, but he needed to leave the child with someone who had no vested interest in the company."

Suspiciously, David protested, "I think that was a mistake. You have come for money."

"Money, David," she corrected him. "I could care less about your silly delivery company."

"I hate to disappoint you, Gabrielle, but thirty thousand dollars is not enough to raise a baby for even one year."

"The specifics as to how I determined that amount, and I think I know what it takes to raise a child. I need enough to get by until I can go back to work?"

"Back to your old job?"

His sarcasm would be hilarious if he weren't so serious.

Stuffing the last of the dessert in her mouth just because it gave her so much pleasure to be selfish, Gabrielle said with a mouth full, "Would you like that?" Standing up, she excused herself to go to the bathroom.

"I possibly would consider it, Gabrielle," David said as she reached the door to leave.

She stopped at the doorway but didn't look back at him, terrified of the molten lust running through her veins. "Too bad you couldn't do anything even if you paid me," she capped and left the room in a hurry to get away from him.

Of course, she didn't have to use the bathroom, but as soon as she got into the closest stall, she let her emotions overwhelm her. She sat on the covered stool, rocking back and forth, taking a deep breath, trying to push aside the sexual yearning fluttering through every vein in her body. She waved her hand to her face to sate the flush building.

Fighting what she was feeling with David was getting harder and harder.

Chapter 12

I know what the problem is

When she returned to the private dining room, David was already standing with his back to her, leaning against the table as if he was deep in thought. Gabrielle cleared her throat, holding at the door, not wanting to get any closer to him.

"Can I ask you a question?" David sounded grave.

"Whether I want you to ask me a question or not, you're going to do what you want, David."

He turned and smirked. "Oliver would slick talk, but I do ask permission. Stop getting us confused." Folding his arms across his chest, he said, "I want to be a godfather in your children's lives, no strings attached. I would do what Oliver was going to do - provide financially - and also be a part of their lives when you allow - including your current son."

Narrowing her eyes warily, Gabrielle asked, "You don't owe my son anything."

"It doesn't matter. He's a part of you, and he would be a sibling to the baby you're carrying. He gets treated equally."

"When you say no strings attached-"

"I mean what I say, Gabrielle."

"Why are you so hell-bent on agreeing before we get back?"

"Because I know it's the last we'll really have a moment alone, where you can think straight - and where I can think straight."

She corrected him, folding her arms across her chest. "Or Mina's not hanging around you or being present."

He shifted uncomfortably. "Neema and I have agreed we need you, and we want you on your terms. We'll sign agreements or whatever you want."

"And when the will is found? Will I be notified if it involves me or my baby?"

Without hesitation, David promised, "You'll be the first to know."

Gabrielle didn't care about the will, but she wanted to see what he was going to say, plus the fact David had thought of Oliver was enormously generous. "I'll think-"

He cut her off, walking to her. "I can't have you think about it, Gabrielle. I have to have your word before we go back to the house that you'll at least allow me to be a part of your children's lives in some sort of way. Supervised or whatever kind of visits, just let me, please, and I'll give you the installments Oliver would have given you however you want."

"You'll be running his company. You'll have all the money you desire."

"No, I have my own money. It's my life savings."

Feeling guilty, she surmised, "For your medical expenses. Why would you give that money up when you need it to live?"

Passionately, David admitted, "Because family means everything to me, and I want to take the mantle Oliver would have wanted me and... what I've always wanted." He reached out his hands and covered her entire stomach. "Whether we like each other or not, Gabrielle, we are what we need." He looked up into her eyes. "We can make this work; if not for us, then the children."

Did he have to be so damn wonderful?

She pushed his hands away. "I couldn't accept your money. I couldn't let you kill yourself."

"My treatments aren't that much," he explained. "If I find... a source."

Noticing how his eyes looked down but then came back up quickly unnerved her. "Please," he begged.

He was right but damn her pride. Couldn't they give her the money and leave her alone?

Yet the many times she wished Charles could have a father figure who could be a positive in his life and now with the new baby... and the fact that David had magic hands.

Just at that moment, the swelling had started to return, and as hard as she tried, she couldn't stop herself from holding her chest.

He knew, though. "You're in pain. I'll help."

"Stop it," she said tiredly, leaning from him against the wall behind her.

"Stop what?" He put a hand up on both sides of her head to stop her from moving away.

Frustrated, Gabrielle weakly pleaded, "Stop helping me, David. Stop being nice. Stop doing everything right."

He raised a brow in amusement. "I'm only doing what I feel is right for you and Oliver's child. I believe you're so used to people not giving a damn you don't know a blessing when it's standing right in front of you, and it's standing right in front of you right now, Gabrielle. Stop looking for a motive and trust. I don't plan on hurting you. You're so damn independent, and you've done things by yourself for so long; maybe it's time you had just a little help. Don't let your pride get in the way."

Closing her eyes as the pain was getting worse in her chest, she couldn't think straight.

David huffed and locked the door before tugging on her hand to guide her over to his chair. "I'm going to help you, so you shouldn't be bothered until later tonight, Gabrielle."

She didn't know how he would accomplish that feat since the discomfort seemed to be coming at least once every hour.

He sat down in his chair with her standing in front of him. "You're going to have to trust me completely."

She allowed him to guide her, so she straddled his legs, but when he started to unbutton her blouse, she held his hand.

"I only want to help you," he said with a promise in his eyes. "I will give you all the relief you want."

It was either this or demand to go back home and bind her chest as tight as possible like she used to do when she was pregnant with Charles.

When Gabrielle released his hands to give him consent, he rubbed his palms together and ordered her to unbutton her shirt. When she started to go past where her bra was, he told her to stop. The area she had displayed to him was enough for him to put his hands inside of her shirt and move his very warm palms under her breast.

"Close your eyes and take a very deep breath... slower, Gabrielle."

When she breathed in, he pressed more in a counter clock motion, and when she breathed out, he lessened the pressure in a clockwise motion. After the fourth breath, the pressure seemed to disappear from the left side, but the right side was still pretty tight.

David seemed to know the left side massage wasn't needed anymore, but he increased the clockwise pressure to the right side while crossing his left hand over his other arm and applying pressure under her right arm.

In three more breaths, she could suddenly feel a lightness and wetness at the same time in her chest area and opened her eyes to see her right breast was soaking her bra. Taking quick action to the letdown, David pulled the bra away to place his entire mouth over her darkened nipple.

She gasped, clutching his shoulders as she felt his tongue move under perfectly to draw out a mouthful of breast milk. Hearing David loudly swallow, Gabrielle wanted to die in morbid embarrassment as he suckled only half a mouthful a second time.

Gently he released her nipple from his lips and quickly covered her up. Reaching on the table, David took several cloth napkins and handed them to her.

Gabrielle could only concentrate on the drop of milk on the side of his lips. She took the napkin and wiped the corner of his mouth.

"Thank you," David said with delight in his eyes. "I'm so sorry for being improper, but you would have soaked your clothes and mine if I hadn't."

"Don't be sorry," she said as she put the napkin inside both sides of her bra just in case anything else decided to leak out. The front of her shirt was still ruined with spots of breast milk.

He noticed this as well. "Do you have an extra bra?"

"Yes," she answered.

"Oliver has some shirts at the condo. We can go back there. They might be a little big, but they should fit fine."

Covering her face with her hands, Gabrielle grumbled in frustration. "That was so inappropriate."

"Gabrielle, it's a pregnancy. It's nothing to be ashamed of," he said with understanding, buttoning up her shirt.

Getting off of him and sitting in her chair, she closed her eyes to gather herself.

David stood up, and she heard the lock on the door click.

When she opened her eyes, he wasn't in the room, and she assumed he went to the bathroom most likely to wash his mouth out with soap.

By the time he returned, Gabrielle had put on her jacket. She was ready to go. The sooner they could get to the apartment, the sooner they could get back to Oliver's house; she could have dinner, sleepover one more night, get her money, and be finished with this family for good.

And Gabrielle swore she would not have another embarrassing situation again!

Unfortunately, she had to admit to herself her chest and whole body did feel freaking wonderful!!

THE TROUBLE WITH GABRIELLE

CHAPTER 13

TAKING FULL ADVANTAGE IN HIS WEAKNESS

And what had happened in the restaurant seem to have been done with once they left.

David did not bring up the embarrassing experience again as they left the restaurant and returned to his car.

"How do you feel?" he asked as they headed to the apartments again.

"Embarrassed," she said. "But I should be asking you how you feel."

"How should I feel?" he questioned, looking at her as they stopped at a light.

Immediately, Gabrielle said, "I'm clean and healthy."

"Good, because I am too."

Why he admitted that to her, she couldn't be sure. "I'm just asking how you feel because this must've been jarring to you."

"Actually, no," he admitted, paying attention to the road. "And it was pleasant that you tasted like dessert - like liquid caramel."

She blushed more, but a text message on her phone distracted her.

Charles let her know he sent the sandwich and other items to the school's forensic lab for his former lab partner, Zuri, to analyze. He then inquired about the steel box in her room by just sending a picture.

Gabrielle replied, "It's from the friend."

"Be safe. I love you," Charles texted back.

"Your son,' David asked as they were pulling into the back driveway of one of the condos.

"Yes," she answered, putting her phone away after letting her son know she loved him too.

David jumped the car, grabbed her overnight bag, and came around to her side to assist her out of the vehicle. Following him inside, he guided her straight to the first-floor bedroom. "There's a second floor, but Oliver pretty much used this to lay his head down and get back to the city."

This room was much smaller than the bedroom in Port Huron, but Oliver didn't need much, as David explained.

David went to the closet and found a shirt hanging up. "There are tank tops in the drawer if you need some." He set the shirt and bag on the bed.

When he started to leave, she said, "I know it's not just the baby that's making you nice to me, David. If that will is never found, you're going to have to do whatever Mina and Neema say for the rest of your life, but if the will is found, you're going to be indebted to me. You don't want to burn any bridge, and I understand."

His back was to her, but she could see he was pressing his hand hard against the wall by the door.

Walking to him, Gabrielle said, "Either way, I appreciate you being nice to me, even if it is to use me later on."

Turning around, David said, You're right. I don't want to burn any bridges because having my family's company in my control means a lot to me. But as I'm getting to know you, I understand why Oliver found you unique from other women and why he gifted you the one thing he knew would be more important to our family. You deserve this and everything wonderful coming because of what you gave."

"I didn't give Oliver anything."

"Yes, you did, Gabrielle. You gave yourself."

Touched by his words, she stood on her tiptoes and kissed his cheek. "Thank you, David."

He excused himself, and she quickly changed from her clothes into Oliver's oversize custom-tailored shirt. The napkins she had taken from the restaurant she kept in the pockets of her jacket instead of throwing them away. The memory of what David had done was just too intimate and just thinking about the feel of his lips on her body made her blush profusely.

The fabric felt purely delicious on her skin, and if she rolled up the sleeves and tucked everything in, she looked a little bit decent. Instead of the pants she wore, she changed to a short black skirt.

Going around the room, she looked at everything of Oliver's and wondered had he returned after their second night together?

Leaving the room, Gabrielle joined David in the kitchen and stopped dead in her step, seeing the familiar-looking beautiful purple plants on the ledge outside of the window. "Those are Monkshoods," she pointed out.

"Mina planted those earlier this summer after coming here to clean up the house when Oliver passed," David said. "It's her favorite plant. She has an abundance in the greenhouse at home."

Gabrielle shivered in fear and asked for a glass of water.

He handed a sealed water bottle from the refrigerator to her, and Gabrielle drank almost half of it.

If the forensic tests come back to say Oliver had any of that in his system, it could be Mina that had killed Oliver? Should Gabrielle tell David?

"How bad does Mina want to be a part of this family?" she questioned as they prepared to leave.

David shrugged. "When her mother first married my father, she followed Oliver and me around like a puppy, but we never paid her attention. She was like an annoying fly. We thought that's what little sisters are supposed to do."

"And now that you're going to be married to her instead of Oliver, won't she expect children?"

David was helping her with her coat, as he replied, leaning over her. "We've found a doctor who can extract enough sperm from me to try in-vitro. It's expensive, but since the natural way is more difficult-"

Turning to him, Gabrielle said, "A woman I worked for used to say it's a mind over matter when it comes to men."

"Really?"

"Yes," she said. "A man has to be in a space in his head to achieve maximum pleasure."

"And you know this from your experience?" he asked, his voice filled with sarcasm.

She shrugged. "I know enough, and I've never had a disappointed customer."

"You're talking to a man who's had every doctor in the world tell him it's impossible, Gabrielle."

"And that's probably the problem. You have every doctor swimming up in your head, but you'd be shocked at what the human body can do."

David gave her a long hard stare before he said, "Could you do it now?"

"I'm a little out of practice-"

"Oh, you were a little braggart a few minutes ago,"

Challenged, Gabrielle took off her jacket, leaving it in the kitchen, and then pulled him into the living room. "Sit," she ordered, taking out her phone and turning on a soft playlist. "You're going to open yourself to me, David?"

"Yes," he said with a shrug.

Gabrielle pushed his knees open and then leaned over to him skeptically. "And you won't judge me when this is over?"

"I have nothing to lose, and I'm very interested in if it's possible. If your theology is true, then we both can be a benefit to one another."

Moving around to the back of the couch, Gabrielle moved on her knees and started a slow massage on his scalp and temple. "Close your eyes, take deep breaths and just tell me everything right now physically bothering you."

It took a moment, but David said softly, "I'm feeling fine."

"Mentally?"

"Too much to say."

She could feel him tense up, and she dropped her hands to his nape and moved around his shoulders before returning to his scalp and temple. Softly, she asked, "Can you imagine a place where you felt ultimately and completely happy?"

"Yes."

The deep timbre in his voice was genuinely relaxing for her.

"Think of that place," she said. "Think of the sounds and the smell of that place."

She saw him draw his bottom lip in slowly as if he were tasting something. Moving her hands lower, he didn't seem to notice with each stroke of her massage; she unbuttoned a shirt.

Her skills at removing a man's clothes seemed to have never gone away, and his breathing was ever so slow and deep. Goosebumps on his skin told her he was in his happy place. With him drawing that bottom lip in between his teeth to lick every once in a while, David was enjoying himself. Coming around the couch, Gabrielle dropped to her knees, continuing to massage from his temple to his chest, while her other hand opened his pants.

His legs were spread apart and gaining access to his manhood was easy. He was soft but hot, and his natural smell reminded her of coconut core. With just a little saliva, she dipped down and pressed in a slow circular motion to his perineum and moved up around the side of his orbs before dropping back down again.

David's head lulled back just as her other hand massaged his neck and moved down to his ribcage, but her other hand entirely held his orbs and manhood. She could feel the muscle twitch, and with a slow breath over the tip, a finger back at the perineum, the twitch turned to a stiffening.

Gabrielle had learned a lot from her "street friends" and knew the magical spots on a man that could give her what she wanted. Bringing a man to fruition was just as exciting for her as it was for him, and for David, this was indeed a conquest she was getting joy from.

"G-Gabrielle," he whispered.

"Shhhh," she said, assuring him, hearing the fear in his voice. "Stay with me, David."

Just like old times, she could hear his body talk to her. Kisses on his waist and his lower stomach; Touches on his inner thighs and all around. His manhood titillated him into building the hardness she needed. Her hands worked him gently and powerfully, kneading and molding his lust to a pinnacle, slowly but surely.

Gabrielle loved watching his body succumb to her will, and intently she watched him shudder as he became harder. Thrilled by her manipulation, she decided to take his libido to the next level.

Yes, this was reckless, but she wanted this one chance to feel David inside of her.

David convulsed and moaned as she let down enough to control his peak, but that was so that she could slip off her underwear. He was far away from reality, and in the world she had taken him to, breathing deeply fully into getting back to his peak.

"Gabrielle," he whispered in awe.

She loved hearing her full name on his lips and quickly moved up. Before he realized her hands had moved away, and her whole body engulfed his manhood inside of her.

His hands came up and gripped her sides so hard, and he looked at her. "No!"

Tightening every muscle inside her around his thickened shaft, she asked, "Do you want me to stop?"

The confusion on his face was mixed with so much lust, David could barely think straight. All he could do was say her name while he moaned, and his hand hands fell away from her side.

"Shhh!" Gabrielle comforted him, moving up and down on manhood ever so slowly while she continued to massage his scalp and temples. "Take me with you, David," she whispered.

Their lips pressed so hard together, she thought they would definitely melt and mold forever. The feel of his tongue pushing between her lips delighted her senses, giving her more secretion as he pumped up inside of her.

David's sexual need was growing stronger. Without denying her, he used one arm wrapped around her waist; he met her downward thrust with an upward motion of his own like a dance he hadn't done in a long time. Initially, his movements were awkward, but she kept up with him until their lustful motions were fluid and perfect for both of them.

His other hand ripped open her shirt and since she only wore the oversize tank top, getting to her breasts was too easy, and it was Gabrielle's turn to cry out in joy as he attacked both breasts, all the while never missing a stroke.

David raised and flipped everything around in one motion until Gabrielle was lying on the couch, and he was over her, masterfully pounding her like there was no tomorrow.

And if the world was ending, Gabrielle wanted to be nowhere else as this man worshipped her with every stroke.

All the while, Gabrielle was half aware her breasts were filling David's mouth with more milk, but he didn't spit it out. He drank with gusto causing a wave of inner pleasure through her stomach, down through her pelvic and thighs. She could feel his thankfulness in his eyes, his kisses, and most of all, his deep loving manhood as his intensity thickened, and she pulled his face up from her breast to thank him with the most tender kiss erotically licking her milk off his lips as well.

David growled and rocked her hips so hard that if she had not been holding on to him, she would have gone off the couch. Their groins were pressed so hard against one another she wasn't sure where she ended or where he began.

Her wince was not of pain, but relief, glory, and happiness as David flooded into her womanhood with his warm essence sending her soul over a beautiful void of bright, beautiful lights and whispers of thank you that repeatedly came from his lips.

THE TROUBLE WITH GABRIELLE

CHAPTER 14

BEAUTIFUL BUT DEADLY

David awkwardly stood and fixed himself before running a perplexed hand through his hair several times. She sat up slowly, adjusting her clothes and taking stock in the fact she hadn't had rough sex in a very long time. Hell, the last man she had been with was Oliver months ago.

"I'm sorry," she said, but her heart was not in the apology. "My hormones took over."

He turned away to compose himself. "I'm sorry too."

"You shouldn't be," Gabrielle said, picking up her tossed underwear and putting them back on. "I took advantage of you."

"I should have stopped-"

Cutting him off as she stood up, she said, "David, I enjoyed myself immensely, and I was apologizing to be polite, but I'm not sorry. Furthermore, I don't want you to be sorry. I started something unstoppable, and no one should ever be bothered by good sex."

Facing her, David blushed, "You sound like Oliver. What happens now?"

She didn't understand what he thought should come next, but she shrugged it off as Oliver had done to her. "It happened, and we go on with our lives. You do what you have to do, and I live my life as I had. We're both two healthy adults, AND it's not as if I'm going to get pregnant. Plus, I'm not a woman to swoon over a guy because I received good sex."

"You're different, Gabrielle," he noted.

"I don't know if that's a compliment or not."

"I've never met a woman like you before, and as I slowly get to know you more, I see why Oliver was attracted to you."

If he continued to speak to her in such a proper way, she wouldn't trust her hormones around him. "I'm going to find another shirt, and then let's hurry back so I can get this night over with," she said, finding an excuse to get away from David.

Gabrielle went to the bedroom to quickly change to another shirt and tossed the other one in the garbage. After freshening up in the bathroom, she joined him in the kitchen. While walking out of the back door with him, she looked over at the Monkshood plants and frowned. Did David know about the poisonous properties of the plants?

Her son texted her just as they were getting in the car again.

"Can you get a sample of the Monkshood? Zuri is saying if she finds the poison, she can compare it with the plant to see if it came from there."

She looked up at the back kitchen window and texted, "Will she be able to come to get it?"

After a moment, Charles replied, "Yes."

"There is some in the back kitchen window of this address." Quickly, she typed the address of the condo on her phone. "I'm on my way back up to Port Huron now to get some samples from the garden they have there."

"Please be careful, Mom," he responded with stress.

"I love you, Charles."

He reciprocated the text, and she put her phone away.

"Your son seems very concerned about you," David noted.

"I'm his only parental unit. He should," Gabrielle said.

"Who do you have watching him now?"

"My mother, but she's only involved unless I pay her. She could care less about my son or me." That reminded her to send the money to her mother's account begrudgingly.

With concern, David asked, "How do you feel?"

"Nice," she said, definitely feeling relaxed from all the oxytocin infused in her system. Turning on the heat and massager on the leather seat, Gabrielle sat back and relaxed for the long drive. "I'm not expecting anything, commitment or anything, David, if that's what you're worried about."

David responded, but her body had fallen asleep in that quick moment, and she didn't hear what he said.

***

The next thing Gabrielle knew, the car was coming to a stop in front of the Port Huron home. Stretching awake, she looked around outside and saw her burned down car was gone from the location, but there was an older model blue Ford Escape.

David had already gotten out of the vehicle and was walking from the other car.

"Do we have guests?" she asked when David returned to open her passenger door.

He handed her some keys. "No, this is for you. It's my old vehicle I had in storage before leaving the states initially."

Gabrielle looked down at the keys and then looked at the vehicle. "You're giving me this car?"

"Seeing that your other vehicle was totaled, I figured you were going to need a new vehicle, and most likely, it wasn't budgeted in what you initially asked for."

Narrowing her eyes suspiciously. "You aren't giving me this because we had sex?"

"No," David said, insulted. "As I said, this was in storage and not being used. The sheriff let me know last night your car was totaled. I arranged to bring my car from storage for you. It's barely used, but it's been kept in great repair."

"Thank you," she said. "I can pay-"

He cut her off, this time passing her the car registration. "No, you won't. You will take the car, and that will be it. This has nothing to do with your decision to let us see the baby or the fact we had sex. I had arranged this last night before anything happened."

She let David help her out of the car and followed him inside.

Neema was excited to see her return. "Thank you for coming back. Mina is just finishing up dinner. Would you like to freshen up?"

The welcome she received today was much different from yesterday, but now that everyone was convinced she was carrying Oliver's child, she hoped she could get her money and get out of there. Whatever David found out, she'd turn it into whatever justice system she could find and decided she should stay away from these people.

She could feel David's eyes on her back, and it took everything inside of her not to turn around and look at him.

Heading to Oliver's room, going down the hallway, Gabrielle noticed Mina's bedroom door was opened. No one was in there, and Gabrielle saw one could walk out to an upper private backyard.

As she entered Mina's bedroom, she paused at a desk in the room. A large photo album opened where pictures of Mina and Oliver had been taken as couples, but it looked as if the woman was replacing them with pictures of David over Oliver. Gabrielle saw in the corner a picture of the nursery Neema had shown Gabrielle yesterday, but there were stickers of pink ribbons all around and the name Mamie in more stickers planted on a pink blanket.

Flipping to the front of the book, Gabrielle saw five large gold letters: G O A L S.

As Gabrielle put the pages back to where they were, she noted Mina had her life goals all planned out, but if she did harm to Oliver, why? It seemed the young woman liked the younger twin more. In a lot of the pictures, Mina could be seen looking at Oliver, and there were a lot more pictures of Oliver than there were of David.

Gabrielle continued beyond the bedroom, where a greenhouse was right outside the balcony going into the house's backyard.

The balcony door was open, and Gabrielle was drawn further into the room. It wasn't the room itself that attracted her but the flowers in the garden right outside the room. The small greenhouse was right outside the balcony, and Gabrielle found herself walking right up to the deep purple Monkshoods.

Remembering her son saying they were poisonous; she used the napkins from the restaurant that had dried out by now and was able to take two flowers. Quickly she folded up the napkin and tucked them into the inside of her coat.

"Careful," Mina said, coming up behind her. "Those are beautiful and deadly."

Pretending not to understand what the woman was talking about, Gabrielle questioned, "You mean these?" She pointed to the Monkshoods.

Mina took her wrist and held Gabrielle's hand to her chest. "Yes, Ms. Gabrielle. I wouldn't want to harm the baby."

Gabrielle could see a look of jealousy clearly in the woman's dark brown eyes.

"Thank you for thinking of my baby, Mina," she said, trying to sound as if she appreciated her concern.

"Well, I have to start now, especially once I become pregnant; we'll most likely put a child lock on the Greenhouse."

"You're going to become pregnant?" Gabrielle questioned, confused. "With David's child?"

"Of course," Mina said. "His father had his son's sperm extracted and frozen. That's why David left because when he came to his father and said he wanted the sperm to impregnate that other woman, his father refused. His father felt that woman didn't deserve to be the mother of David's child." Mina cut her eyes at Gabrielle's stomach. "He and David got into a horrible fight. When it was over, Father sent David away, and David vowed never to come back. He vowed to find another way to become a better father than what he ever had."

"Despite everything that's happened, you look so happy, Mina," Gabrielle noted.

"Why wouldn't I be? Look at your glow! I want that glow. My mother wants that glow for me, and I want to do anything to make her happy."

Gabrielle wanted to let the young woman know it wasn't because of pregnancy; instead, she decided to get to the bottom of Mina. "How long have you loved Oliver and David?"

Mina snorted. "They're my brothers."

"No one just wants to marry their brothers and have their babies," she pointed out.

Pretending to be interested in another plant across the way, Mina said nonchalantly. "It's for the family. I would do anything to help the family."

"I was born last night, but not last night, Mina. I saw the photo album. I see the way you look at David. And I can imagine how charming Oliver can be, but he never spoke of you, and because you were his sister, he didn't turn that charm on you. David's only doing what you're doing out of obligation and family. This can't be the life you want."

Mina turned around to Gabrielle, shooting darts from those dark brown eyes, and was about to say something until Neema's voice interrupted them at the bedroom doorway.

"Dinner's getting cold, girls."

Gabrielle leaned down and smelled the Monkshood realizing Mina's intentions in this whole mess were more prominent than what could be imagined. "Can't be out here looking like a rose when you smell like shit, Mina," she said quietly and quickly left.

Chapter 15

You Owe Me No Explanation

If Mina killed Oliver and now intended to use David, this had to have been a well-thought-out plan. Gabrielle had not been in Mina's path to get what she wanted, and Gabrielle had a feeling Mina would not hesitate to get her out the way by any means necessary.

Charles was right to be very concerned about his mother.

Dropping her coat off in Oliver's room, Gabrielle caught up with Neema.

Neema smiled as they walked down the steps together to the dining room. "You've brought me so much peace, Gabrielle," she admitted.

Mina walked behind them, and Gabrielle could almost feel a heated glare coming from the daughter.

To help increase this animosity, Gabrielle held her stomach like she was big as a house. "I have my next doctor's appointment next month. I could invite you all to come with me. We'll be doing an ultrasound to see the baby for the first time. I could share that moment with you all."

Neema gasped and laughed with joy. By now, they were at the entrance of the dining room, but the older woman stopped and pulled Gabrielle in the tightest hug ever.

"You do not know how many nights of misery I have been through." Tears welled in Neema's eyes as she smiled brightly with joy. "My husband wanted his legacy to live on, and I believe with changing times comes a different way to look at family," Neema continued. "Mina, give us a moment."

Mina looked like she wanted to protest, but she only tight-lipped herself and continued down the hall to the kitchen.

Neema gave Gabrielle another hug. "Thank you so much for bringing this joy to our family."

When Gabrielle was released and was able to breathe again, she said, "Thank you for accepting the joy I bring."

Laughing, Neema said, "I see why You enchanted Oliver. Only sarcasm could deal with his cruelty." She took out an envelope to hand to Gabrielle. "I will never be able to repay you for what you have done to my soul, but whether you agree to have us a part of your life or not, you deserve the peace of mind. We can figure out the details later, but I want to show you how much you mean to me and how much the baby means to us."

Opening the envelope, Gabrielle looked at a private check made out to her for fifty thousand.

"This has come from my private accounts," Neema said proudly. "And after speaking with David about where you live, I agree giving you a duplex with an attached rental property is best. We'll have the lawyer mail you the important papers in your name for the property. You can move your mother in if you want. I understand family is important."

Inside the envelope were keys with a tag of an address. The address she had sent to her son. This was Oliver's old property with the Monkshood. "Thank you," Gabrielle said with gratefulness.

"Now come. Let's eat," Neema said excitedly.

As they walked into the dining room, Mina put a fresh cup of tea by Gabrielle's place setting.

"I made it especially for you," Mina said with a smile. "It's raspberry lemon balm tea. I grew them myself. I've read it's good for pregnancy."

Not wanting to reject this entirely, Gabrielle only smiled in false gratefulness.

Neema and Mina watched her intently as if they were waiting for her to take a drink. All Gabrielle could hear was Charles' voice in her head, "Don't eat or drink anything."

Looking at the cup of hot tea, Gabrielle worried about the life of her baby.

Suddenly, David picked up the cup and replaced it with another cup of tea.

"I think peppermint ginger would be better," he said, smelling like olive soap and roasted chocolate. His hair was partially damp, most likely from the shower he had just stepped out of. "I remember your stomach upset this morning."

He took the other cup, and she watched him put it in the sink before coming back into the dining room to sit at the head of the table. "I've added a carafe on your nightstand as well with peppermint ginger water."

"Thank you, David," Gabrielle said, peeking over the rim at Mina. "It's delicious."

Neema started in on all the changes she was going to make for the upper master bedroom. The excitement in her voice certainly didn't peg her as someone who would harm someone else, but Gabrielle couldn't be sure.

Trust was a big issue with Gabrielle, and she knew her internal struggle was to constantly never believe the shit people were laying down. Taking people at face value and then being disappointed in the latter was always her Modus operandi.

This most likely stemmed from what her mother had done to her for so long. Ingrid only used Gabrielle when she wanted something.

Staring down at the tea, Gabrielle had to admit, David was true to character by looking out for her. And what Oliver had told her about his brother.

There was that sex thing they did this afternoon as well, but it didn't change the fact David still could be friendly to her to deal with her later when he wanted more control of the family business if she was bequeathed Oliver's estate.

For some reason, her eyes strayed over to him, and he smirked because he could read her thoughts.

"Neema was asking you about your afternoon with me? Was it torturous as you thought it was going to be?" David asked.

Shooting her eyes down to her lap, embarrassed by her salacious thoughts and not paying attention to anything Neema had been saying, Gabrielle said, "It was bearable."

"I told David to be on his best behavior," Neema scolded.

"And I was," David refuted. "Gabrielle, don't you agree?"

"He was cordial," Gabrielle responded stiffly.

"I would have joined you both," Neema said. "But along with arranging to get the nursery redecorated, I had to bury Oliver's cat next to him."

This statement caught Gabrielle's attention. "I thought you cremated Oliver."

"Yes, we did," Mina answered. "But there's a family mausoleum where we entomb the ashes. Outside of Oliver's plaque, we had the cat's ashes put in a tube and mounted."

Gabrielle thought this was rather morbid, but Neema explained, "He loved that cat, and to discard it seemed terrible."

"My mother is a sentimental person," Mina said. "When you die, we might entomb even you there."

Despite this being said in a jokeful manner, Gabrielle had a feeling Mina wasn't kidding. She pushed her food around her plate some more, noting her nauseousness seemed to come early.

"Have you thought of a name yet?" Neema asked abruptly.

"I don't like to jinx anything, at least until the first ultrasound," Gabrielle responded. "You know it's there, but you want to be sure, but I have a good feeling this one will be a girl."

Gasping, Neema gripped her chest. "Pink would be beautiful! I haven't done anything with pink in so long."

"And possibly if it were a girl, I'd name her Mamie."

It was Mina's turn to gasp, but Gabrielle only said this after the dig about burying her.

Neema also gasped but with more joy. "That's just perfect. You must know that was Charles Dicken's oldest daughter's name. Mamie stayed faithful to her father until the end."

"Then I think it's just perfect. Otherwise, if it's a boy, it should be Oliver." In exaggeration, Gabrielle rubbed her stomach. "Don't you agree, Mina?"

Stiffly, Mina said, "Too perfect."

Drinking a sip of her tea to hide the quirk crawling on her face, Gabrielle knew the name had pissed Mina off.

"It can't get any more perfect," Neema said. "First the baby and then the wedding next year."

It was Gabrielle's turn to get stiff. True, she had no rights to David, and she didn't expect him to change his whole life just because he had the honor of shanking her in his dead brother's apartment or the fact that he probably hadn't had sex like that in forever.

Plus, Neema had no idea what had happened and was going with the flow. If it did not begin with Gabrielle popping up on their doorstep, life was going to continue as usual unless David changed it.

Gabrielle looked down the table at David, who suddenly found the food on his plate fascinating.

"Yes, Mina, you'll achieve at least one of your goals," Gabrielle said, clearly letting the young woman know she had looked through the photo album. "By this time next year, maybe you'll be pregnant too."

David choked on his food.

Yawning, Gabrielle said, "I'm exhausted. I think I'm going to bed early tonight." As she stood up, David did too.

Everyone, even Mina, wished her goodnight.

Gabrielle was of the mindset to tell the young woman to kiss her back alley on a dark night, but she pursed her lips together and left the room.

Soon as she walked into Oliver's room, she locked her door, didn't bother to turn on any lights, and went into the bathroom. Stripping off all her clothes, she jumped in the shower to wash the day away. The water felt perfect on her skin, and she stood there for a long moment to clear her thoughts.

Touching her stomach, she calmed herself.

Not one moment had she ever thought of getting rid of this pregnancy. She wasn't super religious, but she felt every child should have a chance, and Charles had turned out fantastic, so why wouldn't this baby as well?

Most children received their intelligence from the maternal side anyways and giving Charles a sibling would be incredible.

A large shadow appeared in front of her on the other side of the shower, and she knew it was David who had come into the bathroom.

Turning the water off but not coming out from frosted white curtains, she said, "You owe me no explanation of your plans, David. Sex doesn't obligate you to me in any way."

"I'm not my brother." His hand came in the shower with a large towel.

After wrapping the towel around her body, Gabrielle pushed open the curtains to face him. He was still dressed in his dining room clothes, but did she think he'd be naked?

Yes, she'd wanted that.

Damn.

"It doesn't matter, David. Shit happens; you clean it up and keep it going." She tried to get out of the shower and go around him, but he blocked her path.

"You're not shit, Gabrielle." His eyes drifted down to her chest. "And we certainly can't just clean it up when we both want more from each other."

The thought David still wanted her did excite her, but she knew his condition didn't make it easy for him to have sex even if he desired so.

"What do you want more from me, David?"

"I'd rather show you than tell you," he said, holding his hand out so he could guide her.

She took his hand and let him lead her out of the bathroom into Oliver's room. There were still no lights on, but the bathroom light was just enough as David sat on the bed and moved Gabrielle's body between his legs.

Looking down at him, she watched as he reached up and released the towel. She didn't stop him as his hands moved to gently touch her stomach as if he could feel the baby right there and then.

Seeing the pure fascination with her pregnancy endeared her so much to him. After a moment, his hands moved up to her breasts.

Just like before, he massaged them until she closed her eyes and relaxed, loving the attention his fingers and palms doled upon her.

The feel of his mouth on one nipple made her gasp, and she looked down to see David's mouth wide open, covering her dark areola turned her on. His other hand continued to massage her other breast while his tongue flicked over the nippled and settled underneath, intent on bringing forth the liquidy nutrients. So much was produced, some dribbled from the corner, but he didn't stop. His eyes were closed, and she could see him swallow large gulps while still stimulating her and drawing her body to him.

It was too easy to accept this illicit turn-on, but seeing the enjoyment on David's face made it feel natural and good to Gabrielle.

Her head lolled back as her arms rested on his broad shoulders giving in to his abundant deep suckling, not caring this man was draining any fight from her body. He switched up quickly to the other breast, and there was no doubt this was no mistake.

David was intending on drinking her dry, and she didn't care. Holding her tight, he rolled her onto the bed. Gabrielle's arms fell by her side, but moving slightly, she could easily move to his pants. He was thickened, but in her state of horniness, she was realistic that he couldn't finish. At least she could add enough pressure to pleasure herself.

Being a single mom for so long, she'd become an expert at self-gratification, so at this point, her expectation was low.

Grabbing him by the base, she smiled, liking how he thickened some more. David moved up slightly so she could push down his pants and entwined her legs around him, easily letting his manhood snuggled between her womanly wet lips.

He moved up to look down at her. "This is okay?" he asked breathlessly, filled with worry. "You know I can't-"

Instead of answering him, she pulled his face to hers. Kissing him was powerful, tasting her milky essence still on his tongue mixed with him. This was answer enough for him to moan deep into his body, reverberating down his torso and even making her pelvis tremble. He wasn't fully hardened, but it was enough to press into her.

They both gasped and then smiled into their kiss. Gabrielle didn't want to explore what was to happen afterward or even what had happened before. Right now, Gabrielle wanted to feel worshipped, and David was revering her body with everything he could give her. Her womanhood tightened against him, and Gabrielle's hips shot up to meet every one of his thrusts until her orgasm bursts forth as a dam broke inside of her. Simultaneously, David trembled with her. She wrenched her lips from his kiss and buried her mouth on his arm with her teeth. He only flinched as his mouth found her breast again, giving her powerful aftershocks as he suckled the rest of her milky lifeblood.

What they had created together, she knew no one could tear apart, and for just that moment, Gabrielle wanted to stay in this perfect nirvana with him for eternity.

David raised from the bed and removed the rest of his clothes before coming back to bed. "Let's figure this out in the morning, Gabrielle."

He was saying what she was thinking.

Chapter 16

It was abnormal, but she liked it.

It wasn't the following morning they became aware of their reality. Maybe two hours later. Gabrielle had woken up, but David was already awake.

The room was still dark, but he was holding his head up and looking down at her. The bathroom light gave her ample optics to see his face as he saw hers.

"You don't snore," he noted. "I've never met anyone who slept so quietly."

"You sleep with a lot of people?" she asked.

He chuckled. "Touche'. Usually, people snore."

Feeling her morning sickness starting to affect her, she took a deep breath to push away the nauseousness. "I wouldn't know. I never listen to myself sleep, and I don't sleep with people overnight."

He poured a little tea from the carafe by the bed and handed it to her. "Oliver doesn't seem like the type that would either," he said remorsefully.

"You don't have to feel sorry for your brother," Gabrielle said, gratefully taking a sip. The peppermint worked wonders alleviating her horrible pregnancy symptoms. "He was himself, and that's all I expected him to be. He got what he wanted out of me, just like everyone else does."

David frowned. "Why are you comfortable with everyone manipulating you, Gabrielle?"

"I expect it of people," she said, not at all upset and putting the cup down on the nightside on her side. "My mother kept me around to help her with the bills, cook, and clean for her until I got in her way. Other people I met usually got money or support, and then when I got in the

119

way of their other plans or other friends, they dropped me like a bad habit. Oliver..."

David cut her off. "You don't need to explain anymore, Gabrielle. I understand. You've never had anyone care about you, but it could be different for us. You're fine without another child, which I will most likely never have, and I-"

It was her turn to cut him off. "Let's be honest, David. As soon as you get up and leave this room, you're still going to go about your life and marry Mina. My needs are going to be the last on the list."

He put a finger over her lips. "What I plan to do is to come to some agreement with you, Gabrielle, because Mina can't possibly give me what you give me." He paused. "I won't be like Oliver, but if you want me to be honest, Gabrielle, I-."

Afraid he was going to start spouting some feelings and ruin the moment, she cut him off again, "Really, David, honesty isn't always what it's cracked up to be. We can be okay just not knowing what the future-"

He covered her mouth this time with his grey-tannish brown eyes flashing with annoyance. "You're scared. I understand that. You think I have some false machinations, and I'll say anything to make you stay. That's not the case. I'm a realist like my brother, but unlike him, I feel like we need to establish honesty with each other in terms of this relationship."

She waited a moment before moving his hand away. "There is no relationship, David."

He huffed. "Gabrielle, I'm not going to ask you to marry me, dammit. I do want to continue what we've established, though, yet I want to know if you're comfortable with my situation."

Frowning, Gabrielle moved up slightly so she could look at him directly. "Your health situation?"

"Yes, it is why I have never married." He didn't look down in shame. "With my health condition, my physical ability to get completely erect all the time makes it very difficult for women to understand-"

Leaning over to kiss him, she said, "If I was trying to get pregnant again, David, I guess I would mind. You get firm enough."

His eyes moved to her chest. "But that isn't what excites me."

Her chest reacted to his stare, swelling to fullness.

He continued explaining. "I'm not abnormal, Gabrielle. It's why I went out of the country for treatment. Some believe human breast milk contains cells that can stop the deterioration of organs and even strengthen the immune system."

Gabrielle had to wait a minute as she digested the information and what he was implying. He most likely took her silence as a need to continue to explain.

"My Naturopathic Physician paired me with a harvester that would give me the nutrients, and I can say it works enough. I had more energy, and my symptoms dissipated. I don't need to take a lot of the drugs."

"So you're asking me what?"

He looked up into her eyes, and she swore she was looking at adorable ass Oliver again. "Fresh is best, and I could send a sample to see if you would make a good pairing for me."

"It would mean I'd have to produce double the amount," she said. "With the baby."

"I would make it worth your time."

Getting out of the bed, wrapping the towel around her body they'd drop to the floor last night; she huffed in exasperation. "It's not about the money. That's abnormal; you know that."

"In this culture, it is," he said, sitting up in bed with the covers over his waist. "I want to make sure you understand what I want from you. People use you all the time, and you get nothing from it. And it's not about just what I want from you." He walked up to her wrapping the sheet around his waist. "It's what I need from you, and I didn't want you to get mixed messages from me. Until I can get what I need from a donor, it's an option I need from somewhere. And being close to you, I hope we can come to a monetary agreement to continue helping me."

She didn't know what to think. "It's not about the money. Stop throwing the money at me, David," she said, annoyed.

He stepped back and sat on the side of the bed as if that would alleviate her stress. "Then what can I give you? I'm open to offer anything."

His partially naked proximity was making it difficult not to raise her arousal toward him. Turning away from him to look in the other direction, she said, "I'm not used to anyone asking that of me."

"And because of my physical condition, I do not want you to think you are indebted to me. I understand we all have needs, and I will not be able to fulfill your needs."

She walked out of the room to the bathroom, locking the door behind her.

David huffed loudly in disappointment and came to the door. "Gabrielle, please don't shut me out. Let's talk this out like adults."

Gabrielle didn't answer him for a very long moment. "David, get away from the door and just let me think."

Not wanting to know if he did as she bid, Gabrielle attended to her bladder, brushed her teeth, and just stared at herself for a long moment. His side of the bathroom was open, but she had a feeling David didn't dare leave Oliver's side to come around. True, he would be using her, but he made things worth her time. No one had ever offered her a mutual benefit.

What did she have to lose?

Yes, he was the brother to the father of her child but giving him what he needed while enjoying herself occasionally when he could with his body seemed like a very fair exchange. She was tired of being manipulated and not getting anything from what she sacrificed. David was offering her a chance to be used and entirely without the guilt of enjoying herself.

Gabrielle would be saving his life!... While having nipple orgasms, of course.

What more could a girl ask for?

It took a few more moments, but when she came out of the bathroom, she handed him a disposable cup covered by a paper towel filled with breast milk.

David had returned to the side of the bed where he had initially sat last night. His face was filled with shock but then turned to appreciation. Carefully setting the cup down on the nightstand next to her teacup she had been drinking early, he pulled her in his arms and buried his face in her stomach.

Enjoying the appreciation, she said, "I'll be the mother of two children, David. I don't think I'll have a lot of sexual needs."

She was in line right with his mouth, and she wasn't even sure he heard her last statement as he coaxed her arms down and opened her towel. Pressing her breasts together, he took both nipples in simultaneously and voraciously wrapped his tongue around each one. Gabrielle had begun to enjoy his need for her and the incredible attention he doted upon her. Wrapping her arms around his face, welcoming him closer to her body, she bit her lip, trying to hold back the moan that wanted to escape loudly.

If his hands weren't helping position her breast into his mouth, he was massaging the one he couldn't suckle from while his other hand rubbed her entire backside at the same time.

Gabrielle could feel the gathering in her body as her muscles responded to the sensations internally, and her brain doled out tons of oxytocin. Closing her eyes, enjoying the pulsing, Gabrielle didn't regret her decision. She'd enjoy every moment of this while it lasted.

David was hungry, but the way he suckled long and slow made her lower muscles tighten and release on their own until she felt a natural orgasm generate itself from inside out.

In the fog of her pleasure, she heard a searing gasp behind her.

"You filthy slut!" Mina hissed in disgust at the bathroom door.

Chapter 17

I SHOULD GO

Mina must've come through David's room to gain access into Oliver's bedroom. She was dressed in a sexy nightgown, and Gabrielle could only assume the young woman had most likely entered David's room to seduce him.

Finding her fiancé' latched onto his brother's baby mother was probably not at all what she had expected.

Either way, Mina clearly could see David taking full advantage of Gabrielle, half-naked on the bed.

David shot to his feet, holding the sheet around his waist, and pulled Gabrielle behind him as Mina ran up to attack Gabrielle. Gathering herself, Gabrielle pulled her jacket over her body to cover herself and face Mina.

"She's a harlot, David! How COULD you?!" Mina cried, hitting his chest.

"You don't understand," David tried to reason with her.

They began to shout at each other in Indonesian, but that was just too much for Gabrielle. Finding her shoes, she opened the door to Oliver's room and started to leave, picking up her overnight bag.

"No," David said. "You aren't leaving, Gabrielle. Mina is! Go to your room, sister."

Mina stormed out of the bedroom, saying something very vile to Gabrielle in the other language. David closed the door behind her.

"I should go, David," Gabrielle warned and quickly went to put on her clothes. Standing by the safe, she knelt and opened the first door. Looking at the digital back lock, she said, "Do you know when Oliver programmed this?"

"No, I don't, but he had this all installed about ten years ago."

Narrowing her eyes at the lock, she figured it had to be another day—something his family probably would have never guessed. Entering Charles' date of birth, the safe popped right open, and inside was a large stack of papers.

David had put on his pants by then and rushed over to the safe. "H-How? What was it?"

Gabrielle looked down, feeling upset Oliver left so much in her hands but had told her nothing of his intentions. "Oliver's secret. It was so secret; I don't think he ever meant for any of you to know without me. If I had not gotten pregnant by him and had to come here, we would have never met. This safe would have been locked forever."

"I think he didn't trust anyone to keep his secret safe, except for you, Gabrielle," David explained. "Have you read your letter from him?"

"No," she said.

"You should. I think all the questions about Oliver's intentions and any other answer you wanted to know would be in his letter."

Those words meant more than he knew they meant to her. She gathered things. "I'm still leaving. I know Mina doesn't want me here." She held her stomach for security. "I think Mina would love to get rid of me altogether." Gabrielle proceeded in the hallway, knowing David was following her. "She tends to get rid of things if they get in her way or don't work out in her favor."

David caught up with her just as she got to the stairway and took her night bag, but also grabbed her arm to stop her from moving. "What's that supposed to mean?"

A click at the other end of the hall made them both look down to see Mina had a handgun aimed at Gabrielle.

"Have you lost your mind, Mina?!" David exclaimed. "Put that away."

Gabrielle narrowed her eyes, exceedingly tired of this woman getting away with things. "As I said, David, Mina gets rid of anything that stands in her way. I think she poisoned Oliver and would have poisoned me if I hadn't given the cat my sandwich. Isn't that right, Mina?"

Tears filled Mina's eyes. "I waited years for Oliver! Decades! Saving myself! Sacrificing everything for him and one night with you... YOU FILTHY SLUT... and he comes home with a conscience to say he's not going through with the marriage! And I had to settle on David."

"Oliver wasn't going to marry you, Mina. He was stringing you along to make his father happy until his death, and then afterward, he didn't know how to break it off knowing it would hurt your mother," David admitted. "He told me this in his letter."

"What's the commotion?" Neema asked tiredly, coming out of her room in the hallway before realizing Mina was holding a gun. "Put your father's gun away, Mina." The older woman spoke some words in Indonesian rapidly.

"SHUT UP!" Mina screamed. "You all have no appreciation for how I've waited for my mother to be happy with me." She hit her chest hard with her other fist. "And this bitch comes here and makes my mother happy in one day? She did what I have been sacrificing myself to achieve in ONE FUCKING DAY! I'm tired! I'm tired of being hurt! Of being treated like I don't matter."

Gabrielle rolled her eyes. "You could have walked away any day and made yourself happy, Mina."

"You don't understand family. You have no family. You have no one." Mina put her other hand on the gun to steady her aim at Gabrielle. "But I'm not going to let you take them away from me."

David shoved Gabrielle behind him just as three gunshots went off.

Ducking by the staircase railing, Gabrielle screamed with Neema.

Yet, unlike Gabrielle, who didn't get hit with any bullets, Neema did along with David. Both of them fell to the ground.

"Run," David ordered weakly, clutching his arm trying to get back up.

Mina charged down the hallway, past her mother, and hopped over David, still aiming the gun at Gabrielle.

Gabrielle grabbed the night bag David had dropped and threw it at Mina, knocking the gun away. Mina kept coming, and Gabrielle stood up completely to brace herself to be tackled. They wrestled, and Gabrielle was able to punch Mina in the neck; and the young woman stumbled back towards the stairs but grabbed Gabrielle's jacket, yanking her with her.

The last thing Gabrielle remembered was hoping Charles would be fine as she was pulled down the steps with Mina.

***

From her hair follicles to her toenails - everything hurt. Every time she tried to face reality, the pain would sear through her soul like a knife, and Gabrielle couldn't press on. The darkness felt much better, but she felt the time went by so fast, and she couldn't stay in this unknown realm.

With all her might, she forced her eyes to open to the searing bright light above her face. A slow beeping was annoying, and something was holding onto her hand.

"Gabrielle," a panicked voice said, gripping her hand harder.

"Ouch," she whispered, trying to focus her eyes. She could see the swaggerish large outline near her. "D-David?"

A shadow appeared over her blocking the light. "I'm so sorry. Yes, it's me, Gabrielle."

She could see his beard had grown extensively, but he looked weak, and the whole right side of his body was bandaged. "C-Charles," she said worriedly.

"Who's Charles?" someone else said at the end of the bed.

"Her son," David explained. "I went to the house, but I couldn't get an answer...."

As much as she wanted to listen and get an update on her son, the pain was coming in waves and hitting her body like a pounding lightning storm. "T-The... The baby."

Overwhelmed by so much pain, the darkness pulled her quickly back under, but Gabrielle fought to come back. She had to. Too many people depended on her. This time she couldn't speak. There was something over her mouth. A hissing noise was so loud, along with the constant beeping.

David's voice was shushing her. "Don't talk. They had to sedate you, Gabrielle. You were bleeding out, and your oxygen level dropped very low."

Oh, dear Gawd! She was worried. The baby!

"It's okay," David assured her.

The pain returned. This time was worse than before. She fought to stay awake, but all of a sudden, she felt violent spasms in her stomach. Her baby! She wanted to scream. Her baby!

When she awoke from this torture, she would find Mina and choke the life out of that wicked woman.

THE TROUBLE WITH GABRIELLE

Chapter 18

Too much sleep

When Gabrielle became aware again, little by little, she did a body check. Wiggle toes, stretch fingers, twitch her legs and then take a full deep breath.

Soreness, but no pain.

Slowly opening up her eyes, she had the pleasure of her gynecologist standing at the end of her bed checking her chart. He was an over six five, broad shoulder, good-looking black man that had the unfortunate event of injuring his knee. He then dedicated his life to taking care of women.

"Good morning. I'm glad to see you're awake finally," Dr. Chance Jefferson said, relieved. "And cognizant. I can tell by that initial smirk. It's nice to know my face can still help women smile."

He came around to her side and moved the bed up slightly, so she wasn't lying flat. "I'm sorry about the baby. The fall immediately caused your body to abort the fetus."

Tears filled her eyes as she hugged her waist.

The baby was gone.

Gabrielle was terrified to speak.

Her mouth felt so dry.

The doctor continued explaining. "It was a miscarriage. No other parts were injured, and your bleeding stopped completely in days." Comfortingly, the doctor wiped her tears away. "You needed a lot of rest, Gabrielle, but your vitals have improved tremendously in less than two weeks."

She could care less about her health anymore.

Two Weeks?!

HER SON?

Briefly, she also wondered was David still alive?

Her mouth dropped open in shock, and she tried to speak, but her throat felt like sandpaper.

Chance poured her some water, and she shakily reached for it. Her fingertips felt so numb, and the muscles in her arm felt so weak.

Gently, Chance guided the straw to her lips, but as soon as the water hit her stomach violently, her gut hurled the liquid right back up in the cup.

"Well, that was odd," the doctor said, putting the cup away and going to use the sink in the hospital room to wash his hands.

Looking down at her stomach to ensure she didn't have a bump, she looked at the doctor.

"It could be a reaction to the fact you haven't eaten or drank anything in a while," he said, explaining.

Gabrielle looked down at her stomach again. She did lose the baby, so maybe he could be right.

"It's also been known for women to experience some pregnancy symptoms after losing a baby. You're still producing large quantities of milk despite all our efforts to curb your flow naturally," he said, returning to the bed and starting to do a physical exam on her.

David suddenly filled the hospital doorway, just as the doctor indicated the need to check under her gown.

"Do you mind if he's here?" Chance asked her but cutting his eyes annoyingly at David.

Shaking her head, Gabrielle didn't take her eyes off of David. He was wearing a bandage on his arm, but he was alive.

Chance continued to look in irritation at David. "I'll have to close this curtain if you're going to stay in here."

David only nodded.

With the curtain shut, Chance moved around her body. "The fall was sharp, but you didn't break any bones amazingly. Despite everything, you healed quite fast." He finished his examination and covered her back up, and even put the bed up a little more. "There were sprained wrists, most likely when you tried to brace your fall, but once you're ready, you can get back to work. Your colleagues miss you, Gabrielle."

The curtain shot open by David. "Really? Get back to work, doctor? Are you trying to be funny or stupid?"

Chance frowned. "I don't understand, sir. Gabrielle's good at her job. I've had the honor of seeing her work, and I-"

David swung on him with his good arm, but with Chance being still quite athletic, he ducked away. "You son of a bitch. She's not a whore."

In a swift move, Chance punched David in his good side, but just enough to get the air out of David's lungs, making him hold onto the side of the bed.

"She isn't," Chance agreed. "She works at the hospital in a highly respected position, you idiot. I don't know what you thought she was."

Gabrielle covered her face in embarrassment because her doctor had no idea what her former job was. Holding her throat, she whispered, "Forgive him."

"Oh, most definitely," Chance said, checking the damage he'd done to David, but David snatched away from the doctor.

He went to the door where he'd put a paper bag he'd brought and returned to Gabrielle's side and took out a to-go cup. She could immediately smell the peppermint, ginger honey tea and reached for the cup hungrily.

"Please be careful," Chance warned. "Her digestive system is still fragile."

The ginger was strong, but the honey helped her throat pull the warm liquid down, and she closed her eyes in satisfaction, glad to get something in her body.

Chance asked to examine the tea.

"I'm not trying to kill her," David sneered.

"I just don't trust you, sir," the doctor snapped. "The cops did find the poison in your stepsister's room that killed your brother."

Gabrielle gasped. "You know?" she asked David.

Chance answered for David, "Of course he knows. He helped get Oliver's ashes examined where the poison was discovered, and tiny remnants were found in the cat as well. Seems like the feline had been eating some of Oliver's food."

David continued explaining, "Over a two-month time, Mina had been slowly poisoning Oliver." He stopped for a moment looking in pain. "I believe Oliver suspected something but a little too late, unable to prove his suspicions which was why he made it so difficult in the end and trusted only you."

Taking over, Chance said, "If we had not found out what poison was used, most likely no one would have suspected anything or even believed what you had revealed."

"H-How ... how did you find... t-the poison?"

"An anonymous envelope was delivered to the county coroner's office the day after every happened," David answered. "Someone had written a thorough report including Oliver's hair and preserved pieces of a sandwich, plus the poison from the flower grown at the Detroit house was in there and matched with the poison found in Oliver's ashes."

She gasped. "C-Charles."

David looked down in disappointment. "I don't want you to get worried, Gabrielle, but I've had someone go by the house every night before I come to the hospital, but no one's answered the door. We finally had to do a well-being check, and the house was empty. No furniture, none of your items - nothing. Someone cleaned out the house, but none of the neighbors saw anything. I couldn't find your mother or a way to contact her. No one's seen your son, and no one has answered the door in the past month, but someone did take the envelope I left in there."

"What e-envelope?" she demanded to know.

Sheepishly, David admitted, "When I came over to drop you off, while you were inside, I left thirty thousand dollars in an envelope for you to discover when you returned."

"But ... N-Nee..." She had to drink some more tea to finish. "Neema gave me a check."

"I know, but I felt that wasn't going to be enough to help you get on your feet with the baby and a ten-year-old. And despite everything, I want you to keep that money from Neema as well."

Chance snorted.

David didn't know how much she made as a surgical assistant, but she wasn't going to explain her career when she needed to stress her voice out on what was important.

"We have the police looking for him," Chance assured her. "We found graduation pictures, and even some of your co-workers found current pictures of your son in your locker. They issued the Amber alert a week ago."

Of course, she was going to be worried. Gabrielle had been in the hospital for over a month, and no one could find her son or her mother?

Charles could take care of himself. Unfortunately, her mother could have gotten the envelope, sold all Gabrielle's stuff, and left town. Yet, if Charles had found the envelope left in the mailbox and didn't feel safe with Ingrid, he most likely took the money, packed up all their personal and essential items, and was hiding out until he could find his mother.

"My phone," Gabrielle demanded.

"It shattered in the fall, and there was no SD card on the phone. The hard drive couldn't be extracted from," David said. "Since it was paid as you go, they didn't keep phone logs."

That was her fault because she had to downsize to pay for cheap phone service. Putting her son through the top schools, making sure he had the best educational foundation for his learning level, was more critical, and she had put all her money towards Charles.

"I-I can't stay here," she insisted, needing something to distract her from being depressed about losing the baby and her son. "I need to be... be out looking for my son," she insisted.

"You and I both know you need to recover," Chance protested. "At least a couple of more days?"

"What if I promise the care she needs at her home?" David offered. "I can have a nurse come to attend to her twice a day and then be by her side at night as I have been doing."

"I-I can't ask that of you," Gabrielle protested.

"You don't have to, Gabrielle. And As for your son, I made a promise to you to be his Godfather, whether you had the baby or not. I've pushed all my resources on locating him. We're going to find him, but I need you to rest so you can be here when we bring him home to you," David insisted.

Protesting, Gabrielle said, "I can't live in that house in Port Huron."

"It doesn't matter. The house is yours, but you can stay in Detroit in the condo that's yours already too. Neema managed to sign everything over to you once she got out of surgery, and the will Oliver left that was in the safe clearly states he left everything to you, but once all this debacle is figured out, either way, the property will be yours."

"Neema died?" She covered her mouth to hold back her upset. Crying would make her stomach hurt.

Mina had hurt so many people.

David sighed, sounding as if it were difficult to speak. "She made it out of surgery. After the lawyer left, she bravely asked about what Mina had done. When I told her, she... she just slipped away that night in her sleep." He took a deep breath. "I believe she already knew the betrayal when she awoke from surgery, which was why she changed her will. She didn't want Mina to get anything."

Bravely, Gabrielle questioned, "And Mina? What happened to her?"

David looked at Chance, who nodded to proceed. "She's a paraplegic in a criminal hospital upstate. She'll never walk or talk again, but when it's all said and done, she'll serve the rest of her life in prison for the death she's done."

Taking a sip of tea, Gabrielle touched her stomach. This hadn't been the baby's fault. Mina had started her destruction when Oliver came back from seeing Gabrielle the second time to say he wouldn't marry Mina.

Yet, the woman had been insanely obsessed for decades. Oliver couldn't have known the extremes Mina would have gone to when he decided to be happy.

"I'm sorry about your brother," she said to David.

"It's not your fault, Gabrielle." He looked at the doctor. "Do you think she can get her exit papers today?"

"I'll have the nurse draw blood and another urine test." Chance didn't look like he wanted to. "Once those are analyzed, we could have her home by this evening."

She relaxed and gave David an appreciating smile.

Chance checked his pager. "I have more rounds, but I'll be back to check on you, Gabrielle."

After the doctor left, David situated a chair by the bed.

"You aren't leaving?" she questioned.

"No, I've taken the day off at the office, now that you're awake, and decided to spend the day with you. No need for you to spend your first day up in a long time by yourself."

She smiled. "Thank you, David."

Leaning to her gravely, David said, "Don't thank me so soon because you might hate me after I tell you something that I couldn't tell you in front of the doctor."

THE TROUBLE WITH GABRIELLE

Chapter 19

Oh Where Did My Little Boy Go

Just as he was about to speak, a nurse came into the hospital room. David stood up and turned around while the nurse did an exam, collected blood, and used the catheter to collect urine samples.

"This should only take a couple of hours before we know the results, Ms. Payne. Surprisingly, you sound healthy, and there's no bleeding occurring anymore," the nurse said.

David said, "If you could also arrange for a home nurse as well and let me know how I can add my credit card to her account to cover expenses, I would appreciate it."

"We'll see after we get clearance about getting your exit papers," the nurse assured them and then left.

The anxiousness was barely keeping Gabrielle contained because she needed to know why she would hate David and what couldn't he tell her in front of the doctor?

When the nurse had left them, David sat back down and held out his hand. "May I hold your hand, Gabrielle?"

She liked that he asked permission. His palm was warm, and he caressed the top of her hand before kissing her knuckles.

"When you gave me your sample, I sent it in. You're a perfect match, my doctor determined. I was glad because I was running low, and I knew my immunity would suffer if I didn't keep up the same levels."

Gabrielle waited with bated breath as he continued.

"Since you had given me permission, I felt even though you were recovering, you wouldn't mind if I continued your flow," he admitted.

Looking down at her chest, she could see her breasts were well bound but full. In a couple of hours, she would have to nurse or suffer the pain.

"I told the hospital you didn't want any chemicals, and once you awoke, you would stop your flow on your own. I know you didn't make these provisions, but they couldn't ask you, so they just took my word. All the while, I've had to come in here at night to pull ice bags off your chest, warm you up, and relieve the pressure."

She didn't know if she should be angry or not. "You stole my supply, and now you still want that from me?"

"Not only do I want your supply, but I need it, Gabrielle," he said emphatically. "The question is if you want to continue. I know it's difficult with you losing the baby."

It was her turn to press her fingers against his lips to quiet him. "You're right; it's hard, but I think I should still help you, David, as you've helped me."

David pulled her fingers away and smiled. "Thank you, Gabrielle."

***

"Momma!"

She heard Charles call out.

Everything was so dark, and as much as she stretched her eyes open, she couldn't see anything around her.

"Charles!" she cried out.

Footsteps were running to her, and she could feel someone holding her, but she pushed them away because they were pulling her away from the direction Charles' voice was coming from.

"Momma!" Charles called very far away.

"No! No!" she cried, fighting whoever was holding her.

"Gabrielle," David said, pulling her out of her sleep. She looked up at him, seeing a fresh scratch on his neck.

"I'm sorry," she said, knowing that was her damage.

They were in the queen size bed in Oliver's bedroom of his condo. David was topless, still soaked from a shower. His hair was damp all over his body, but he had managed to put on some boxers. "It's fine," he said. "Are you okay? I heard you screaming from the shower."

"I'm good." Her stomach rumbled.

"You're hungry." He kissed her forehead. "Let me dry off and finish warming up dinner."

Being home from the hospital just as David wanted by that night, she was still relatively weak, but her attraction to David was still high.

He moved off the bed but then looked back because Gabrielle hadn't let go of his hand.

Moving back to the bed, David pulled her in his arms. "It's okay to be sad," he said.

Hearing his permission pulled at her heart. Gabrielle was holding back, and she completely relaxed, closed her eyes, and let the sadness fill her. Tears welled in her eyes and ran down her cheek.

Gabrielle could feel his arms tighten around her body, and it was just what she needed. As much as she tried to deny David didn't mean anything to her, he filled a void she had long to hope a man would.

Yet, she was terrified of depending on someone, letting them manipulate her, and then leaving her.

Still, the proximity of having his body molded against hers at this point and time felt ridiculously incredible. With the bit of joy she had been feeling lately, she relished every millisecond.

David unconsciously rubbed her back while he spoke, "I sent the list you made with the description of your possessions to local pawn shops to see if anything had been turned in."

"There wasn't much value to anything. Other than my son's computer and I'm distressed about the plants he was growing in his room for his various projects, I didn't have anything of value."

"No jewelry?"

She shook her head. "Everything I owned, if it was valuable, I sold it to pay for my son's private education. I wanted to make sure he had the best footing in life."

"Understandable."

Looking up at him, she asked, "Do you really understand, David? I've worked so hard to give Charles a good life, and the baby would have derailed everything without Oliver's support. I wasn't trying to be a gold digger. I just needed to get ahead before I drowned and failed as a mother."

"Yes, I know how hard it is for African American women, especially single mothers, to get ahead in this world. I've seen the injustice. I'm not blind to what is out there. I also know from what you've said about how your mother wasn't there for you and failed you that you don't want to be anything like her. I admire you for doing what you have to do, but I feel a little bad for you that no one's given you a nice necklace or earrings to compliment your beauty."

His words cause her heart to skip a beat. He had been listening to everything she had said, understood what she had gone through, and that meant a lot. "I never asked for stuff from anyone, plus I've been so involved in work and raising my son, I rarely dated."

David looked skeptical. "I find it hard to believe men didn't want to date you."

Blushing, Gabrielle responded, "It's not that I wasn't asked, I just didn't have the time, and it would be wrong of me to ask someone to commit to me when I had other commitments."

"Like your son," he determined.

Her stomach growled loudly again, and she cringed, embarrassed.

David chuckled and said, "I'll get dinner finished and bring it to you."

"I can come to the kitchen," she offered.

"No, the doctor and the nurse were adamant about you staying off your feet for at least a day." He nodded to the small card table and the chair he'd set up in the corner of the room. "I don't want that doctor finding out you strained yourself on my account."

Unconsciously, he kissed her brow and left the room.

For the first time in a long time, Gabrielle rested by laying back down in bed. On the way home from the hospital, David had contacted the detective in charge of her son's missing case. She was assured the department was working desperately to find him.

When they had arrived at the house, David helped her get to the bathroom, and she took a long shower, washed her hair, and double-brushed her teeth. David had several thick nightgowns for her to choose from, and a nice light blue one just lifted her spirits after the long hot shower. Gabrielle finger-combed her hair and was able to pull two decent French braids, but she could feel the strength in her hands weakening from no use for so long.

In the back of her mind, she was very worried about her son, but she was oddly calm for right now. As if staying with David, everything was going to work out.

Where Ingrid had disappeared to, Gabrielle couldn't think of a place.

After leaving the hospital, David also helped her discover that her mother had lost her home and stayed temporarily with some friends.

David had found these friends on social media and was told they'd kick Ingrid out because the woman had stolen from them as well. Gabrielle now understood why her mother had readily accepted taking care of Charles and why her mother kept demanding money.

As for all her items in her old house, including the steel box, Gabrielle couldn't imagine where everything had disappeared to.

Like she told David, none of her items, other than the newly acquired steel box, was worth anything, but she kept things in good condition. Her son had no reason to think they were living on thrift store furniture and bought items at low-cost stores and in bulk to save every dime.

Her stomach growled again. Looking at the digital clock by the bed, Gabrielle thought it was odd that her body was still on her pregnancy cycle. When she was pregnant, she could only eat between eleven and six p.m.

At least she wasn't suffering physically from the stress of losing the baby. She had to thank David for that. With the lactation, he continued to induce her uterus had eased itself back in place, and her period had dwindled fast. Physically, she only felt weak from being in bed too long, but she would let David spoil her for today and then get herself up and about to look for her son tomorrow.

Getting snuggled under the covers as she waited for David to return with dinner, she heard the doorbell ring, and a few minutes later, David entered the bedroom with a tray full of food and a replaced cell phone.

He put everything at the table and then came over to the bed. Without straining, he lifted Gabrielle to carry her over to the table.

"I really could've walked," she protested.

"You could've but let me spoil you, please," he said. "The only thing they said I'm allowed to let you do on your own is to use the bathroom and shower."

She took the napkin from the tray and placed it in her lap, rolling her eyes in exasperation.

David handed her the phone. "This was just delivered by one of the delivery drivers. He picked it up for me." He placed the new phone in her hands. "The bad news is that your number was lost since there were no minutes added to it. The good news is that you're a smart cookie, according to the phone store employees, to connect your email contacts to your pay-as-you-go phone. All you have to do is sign in, and you should be able to pull up any numbers you saved to the cloud."

Her heart skipped a beat as she scrolled through the contacts. She could contact her mother, and now she could call Charles IF he had minutes on his phone. Usually, she would do this at the beginning of every month, but since she had been out for almost a month, if her son did not add his minutes, his phone would be dead, and his number would be lost as well.

Getting to Charles' number, her fingers almost shook as she pressed the button to call him, and she waited to hear if it would say the number was disconnected or it would ring.

Dear Lord, please protect my son, she prayed. Please bring him back to me safe and sound.

The phone rang for the third time. Still no answer.

Chapter 20

Let him Drink

On the fifth ring, the phone went into the generic computer voicemail.

Gabrielle left a voicemail just in case this was still Charles' number. "Hi love, it's your mother. Call me back on this number. I was in the hospital, but I'm at the house where I gave you the address. I'm so sorry, Charles. Please let me know you're okay."

Reluctantly she hung up the phone. If it weren't Charles' phone number anymore, some stranger wouldn't come knocking at the door."

"You sound so formal," David commented, taking the two covered plates of food off the tray before setting the plastic-coated trays aside.

"If you met Charles, you'd understand why. My mother said he was too grown." She flinched, thinking about both of them and still wondering where they had gone.

"Do you think your mother would have kidnapped your son?"

Gabrielle shook her head very sure. "My mother was only there because Charles is at an age where neighbors like to call the police about single mothers who leave their kids alone, but in truth, Charles is mature enough to take care of himself."

"I have the drivers stopping at various pawn shops on their routes around your house to look for items you listed of value, including the steel case, and no one's reported anything."

Slumping her shoulders in disappointment, she said, "I'm praying Charles would go where he would know he was safe and not with my mother."

"You've never sounded fond of her," David noted.

Her throat went dry as she reminisced about her mother's ill-treatment her whole life. "Ingrid is not someone who cares about anyone but herself. She'd do whatever it took and take whatever she wanted to get ahead in life and won't care who she hurts in her way."

"I take it you're referring to yourself."

"I wouldn't have left my son with her if I knew I'd known I would be in a coma for almost a month."

David reached over the table and covered her hand. "I'm sorry for all you've been through."

"It's not your fault, but I will blame your brother. I'm not mad, just terribly worried about my son. His school just sent me an email to let me know he took his finals early two weeks ago and has not returned to school, but the good news is that he renewed his following year with the same address. I was able to change his address at school, and maybe that would help give him a clue where I am located."

"I do have to ask, why'd you name him Charles?"

She tried not to hesitate when she responded. "I was always fond of the name Charlie." This was a half-truth. "But when Charles learned how to spell his name, he demanded not to be called Charlie." She wasn't going to tell David this was when her son was three.

Picking up the fork to start eating her food, she found it difficult to cut the meat despite the tenderness. Her hand strength hadn't returned fully, and David noticed her difficulty.

Taking a sip of his wine and then wiping his mouth, he got up and moved behind her. She hadn't put the fork down, and instead of telling her to do so, David's hand came over hers, and with his other hand, he picked up the knife.

He concentrated on cutting up her meat while she focused on controlling her sexual urges. How could she feel horny after everything she had gone through? Turning her head to him as he was finishing up, he looked at her too.

Those sultry grey-brown eyes brightened. David could feel her attraction and didn't move away as Gabrielle pressed her lips to his.

He released her hands and turned her around in the chair. He deepened the kiss by tilting her head back, making her part her lips and join his tongue. She became instantly dizzy as her lust for him increased.

Oliver could physically make her want him, but there was something about David that made her feel an exhilarated rush on her soul. Yet, as this was so new, she wasn't sure what to do.

She encouraged him by wrapping her arms around him and moaning her need.

"Are you sure?" he asked worriedly.

Gabrielle was thinking the same thing about him knowing his health restrictions. "Shouldn't I be asking that of you?"

"Your medical condition is more prevalent than mine at this time, Gabrielle."

"How about this?" she suggested. "If either one of us... can't...or don't feel comfortable..." She blushed because she didn't know how else to describe what she wanted to say, then we can say, "Apples."

She only said this word because there was a bowl of fake apples in the middle of the table.

He relaxed and noted, "I do hate apples."

"Perfect," she said. "Because I'm very much sure."

David didn't hesitate to continue kissing her while he scooped her up and carried her back to the bed.

Voluminous levels of joy filled her, increasing her arousal and longing for him. Running her fingers through his hair, loving the softness on her interdigital folds, and pressing his mouth on hers, coveting their ocular connection, Gabrielle was very ready for anything.

When he laid her on the bed, his topless body shortly followed to cover her. Gabrielle moved her hands down to open his pants.

She waited for him to stop her or call out a safe word, but he didn't, even when she gripped the base of his shaft. He was thickening, and at her touch, his manhood flinched to let her know how happy her touch made him. She loved hearing his body speak and was encouraged to push the boundaries.

Nudging him onto his back, she left off the bed and pulled down his pants.

David didn't protest. He assisted her in becoming fully naked. Standing over him, she admired the beauty of his body, noting having hair, unlike Oliver, just made David sexier.

Starting at his calves, she touched his body, almost worshipful, loving the feel of his skin and just the tone. Gabrielle enjoyed how his breathing would change when she went over a sensitive spot. David let her take her time, while Oliver had been one to rush her or take over.

David languished in her touch, and this aroused her more.

His dark peanut-colored natural tanned skin was beautiful as she ascended to his muscled thighs, over his waist, and to his chest, slowly rolling over each inch of skin. David would try to watch her but become so consumed by her touch; he had to close his eyes and luxuriate in the feel before forcing himself to watch her again. He was fighting his lust but allowed her to indulge in touching him.

As she descended, she planted wet longing kisses down his chest, to his stomach, along his waist, and around the meadow of soft dark hairs at the base of his shaft. Gently she orally nursed each orb individually, wrapping her tongue around before releasing and attending to the other, and then she nibbled on the sides of each thigh before conquering the now hardened shaft, twitching and almost shouting for attention.

Avoid touching his shaft for this long was what she had done on purpose, knowing whether he was restricted or not, that this part of his body would clamor for any and all attention. When Gabrielle finally, ever so softly, licked around the rim, David released a loud groan and threw his head back.

Her licks became carnivorous nibbles all over the tip, and then she drew him over her tongue, down her throat until he pressed internally near her collarbone.

David yelled something in his language and sat straight up. She could imagine his shock of being engulfed by a woman without her gagging, and this most likely had never happened to him.

Feeling his warm essence run down her throat, she wasn't worried because his manhood could stay hard enough to give her pleasure all night long.

That was one thing Oliver couldn't do. Once he was done, he was finished, but David... because he couldn't ejaculate a lot, he could still maintain his semi-hardness to give her pleasure.

Smacking her lips, she crawled up on him, straddling his waist and taking off her nightgown. David lovely caressed her shoulders, languished over her breasts, and moved his hands down her stomach over old stretch marks and around her full hips. Sitting up, he pressed her chest to his and kissed her deeply.

Gabrielle had to fight not to fall in love with this man at that moment.

He accepted and adored her completely.

Pushing him back down on the bed, reluctantly breaking the kiss, Gabrielle lowered her body over him. "Are you hungry?"

David fervently licked his lips, and his fossil-colored eyes danced enthusiastically.

Rolling her over onto her back simultaneously, David attached his mouth to her entire aureole and hungrily suckled.

"We have all night," she assured him, caressing his face, loving how he pulled her warm milky essence in large mouthfuls into him.

The dopamine had started to kick in, and Gabrielle laid in strong heavenly arms, letting her lover take from her, feeling so good all over. She would attend to her other needs much later, but for now... she would let him drink.

Chapter 21

What's Wrong With You?

Opening her eyes the following day before the sun rose, Gabrielle could feel him still behind her, resting on her shoulder blade in a deep sleep. She stayed in bed just for a moment to relish the feel of David's deep breathing, wondering what would happen if she allowed herself to fall in love with him?

Crawling out of bed without waking David, she went to the bathroom to relieve her bladder and wash up. They had taken a shower after hours of lovemaking, and then David had given her the top to his pajamas, which she had put back on in the morning.

After she finished in the bathroom, Gabrielle went to the kitchen with her phone to check her messages and email.

Nothing from Charles.

Gabrielle checked the digital local obituaries and police blotters, but nothing sounded like her son or her mother.

Suddenly, she felt the nauseousness take over her, and she was running down the hall throwing up.

Her breasts swelled so hard, and she had to hold her chest as she emptied whatever she had eaten all of yesterday.

What the hell?!

She wasn't pregnant anymore, so why would she still have symptoms?

Sending an email to her doctor, she figured Chance would respond once he was in his office and give her the results of her blood work.

Could there be more wrong with her from the fall?

Maybe her brain had shifted? Perhaps something wasn't right in her body?

Sitting on the edge of the bathtub, Gabrielle stressed because she didn't need her health to be in danger while her son was missing.

Rinsing her mouth out thoroughly with mouthwash several times, she moved slowly so her emotions wouldn't disturb her stomach again as violently.

Struggling to the kitchen, she found the peppermint tea David had lovingly stocked for her.

She went through the motions of making the tea. On the counter beside the stove was the case for the breast bump. While the water was warming up, she cleaned everything and set the case on the couch to get her mind off the problems overwhelming her brain. After her tea was made, she sat on the couch, hooked the double pumps to her nipples, and relaxed.

The mechanical motion wasn't as gentle as David's, but the machine worked swiftly to fill up four bags while she drank her tea.

This helped stave off the urge to throw up, all the while keeping her mind off of the terribleness of the situation she was feeling.

Just as she put the bags in the freezer and cleaned up the pump, David appeared at the kitchen doorway with only the bottom of his pajamas. The clock was striking seven in the morning, and the sunrise had just occurred on the Detroit Riverfront.

"How do you feel?" he asked.

His kindness touched Gabrielle. "I find it amazing that you ask me that when you're in the situation, you're in."

"I take care of myself. I've done this all my life." David shrugged and came over to her. Pulling her passionately in his arms, he kissed her. "It's you who lost a baby and has no idea where her son could be, but you look good."

She knew he was trying to cheer her up with the compliment because she'd only patted down her hair, rinsed off, and brushed her teeth. "I am good," she agreed, moving away.

"So, who was throwing up about an hour ago?"

"It could be an after-effect," she explained.

"Did you contact the doctor?"

"I sent an email."

This relaxed David as he started to make coffee and toast.

The doorbell rang, and they both looked at each other, wondering who that could be.

"Get in the bedroom," David ordered in a whisper, moving to his jacket hanging up by the door and pulling a nine-millimeter from the inside pocket.

Moving to the living room corner by the long hallway, she continued to peek around the corner, watching him intently.

He quietly approached the door, holding the gun down and looking through the peephole. Looking back at her, David shook his head to indicate he didn't see anyone.

Gabrielle hadn't turned off the porch light from last night, so she was sure he would've seen anyone out there if they were still standing on the porch.

David opened up the door and looked down the street. No one was around, and this bothered Gabrielle more.

When he closed the door and returned the gun, she asked, "Is that firearm licensed?"

"Yes," he assured her.

"Are you sure Mina's a quadriplegic in a criminal hospital in upper Michigan?"

"Positive. Unfortunately, since I'm her only relative, I'm given constant updates about her criminal trial, which she can't attend because they cannot move her until they're assured there won't be any harm to her spine," David said.

"That mean she's able to stand trial? Can she communicate? Is she awake?" Gabrielle asked in a panic.

"Yes," he said gravely. "Not well, but enough, the doctor deemed her competent to stand trial." He walked up to Gabrielle. "I had the option to wait until she could heal better, but I think she needed to pay and put this all behind us as soon as possible. And it's not just because of you, Gabrielle. She killed my brother and her mother. She's most likely in her type of hell and wants this over with as well, so she's not constantly being reminded of what her hate has done to so many people."

Gabrielle relaxed a little bit more. David was automatically kind, so she couldn't be mad at him for making decisions for a woman he felt was his sister.

David said, "Now about your son. How far are you willing to go to find him?"

"As far as possible," she said. "Charles can take care of himself, but he needs to be with me."

"Would you be willing to go on the news? I know you've filed a missing person report, but I think we need to go a little further. I have a couple of friends who could get in contact with some local journalists."

She was shocked David was helping her so much. "Are you helping because you think I still have some hook into your company?"

He looked initially confused by her answer but then amused. "No, Gabrielle, I'm helping you because I love you."

The confession threw her off, and she even had to take a step back because of how the words rocked her soul.

How long had she waited for any wonderful man to say those words to her?

How long had she felt no one would ever say those words to her?

And now, this man was confessing love.

"W-We only just met, David," she said with hesitation because she still couldn't believe he had said those words.

David was standing an arm's length away. "I don't need ten years to know if I love someone, Gabrielle. I know my heart, and I know what I want and need. I love you, and I don't need you to say it back. I'd appreciate it if you could let me know if my words have affected you."

Looking into those beautiful murky tannish eyes staring intently at her, Gabrielle almost trembled. "Yes, they have, David. Thank you." Her fear kept her from saying anything about her feelings.

She'd been a single mother too long. Always by herself. Constantly struggling and being disappointed in the world because no one wanted to help her.

Now there was this man. A man that looked like the man she had given a baby to who she wished would love her, but his brother was loving her. Was she wrong to keep her feelings away from David? Was she feeling guilty because she lusted over Oliver and hated that David, her baby daddy's twin, loved her the way his brother should have loved her?

Damn!

Chapter 22

There's Something Wrong With Him

In an hour, David drove her to a couple of reporters who immediately took her story and did an interview with her, promising to post it by noon or six o'clock on television and by the next day in print. She made sure she hinted her son could find her where she told him to go in the interviews. Charles would understand the address in the last text message, which could lead him back to her, and she prayed her son understood the overt message.

Right after her last interview at noon, the doctor sent her an email and asked if she could come in tomorrow morning to discuss her test results, but also asked if she could stop in today to his office to do another drop.

David didn't mind driving her around, and when they returned to Oliver's place, Gabrielle smiled, seeing the vehicle he'd given her out at the family's house parked in front. David had an extra key to the car and unlocked the doors to reach under the seat to get the primary keys. He gave them both to her, and she hugged him excitedly, forgetting they were in public.

He didn't look uncomfortable at all, which she had expected from Oliver. David enjoyed it and kissed her in reward. They went inside, where shortly after dinner was delivered.

"You're spoiling me," Gabrielle said as they sat down to dinner.

"I have to get to work tomorrow, and you need to rest." He kissed her forehead and began to enjoy the meal.

A knock at the front door came again, and this time the doorbell rang also.

They looked at each other suspiciously.

Automatically Gabrielle got up and went to the beginning of the hallway to hide while he went to the door and retrieved his gun. He peaked out the door and then looked back at her with confusion.

"Who is it?" he asked loud enough for the person on the other side of the door to hear.

Someone muffled back a name, but Gabrielle was too far away to hear anything.

Whoever it was, David put the gun away and opened the door.

Her son flew past David and found his mother giving her a hug that knocked the breath from her body.

"Charles!" she screamed, holding her son and then falling to her knees to hug him so hard.

He looked well taken care of, albeit needing a haircut to his black naturally curly hair. Unfortunately, he was still wearing the same clothes Gabrielle had last seen him in, but they weren't dirty; they just smelled of harsh soap like they'd been hand washed but not rinsed out thoroughly. His skin was dry, and he looked a little dehydrated. They were both crying, and it felt like they hugged for hours, just not saying anything.

"Where were you?!" Charles demanded to know. "I looked everywhere!"

"I was in the hospital. I lost the baby, and I was knocked out for a long while," she explained. "You know I'd never leave you, my son. Where have you been?"

"Around," Charles said evasively. "When you didn't come back after two days, and I couldn't get ahold of you, Grandma said if you didn't come home by the next day, she would turn me over to the state. I got scared, and that night I packed up everything valuable I could carry and left. I got my friend Zuri, who was helping me with the flower research, to help me. She was my lab partner, remember?"

"You sent the folder to the police with the evidence?" she asked.

"Yeah. Well, I got Zuri to do it in case they had any questions. I knew they weren't going to believe a kid." He looked past her to David, leaning on the wall nearby, looking tenderly at them.

Gabrielle drew Charles' attention back at her not wanting David to get a really good look at Charles face. "And after that?"

"Well, I didn't want anyone knowing I was homeless because... well, you know, Momma."

She agreed, "I understand. So where have you been?"

"Hiding at the school. I found a good hiding place for our stuff, and then I found different closets all around I could sleep in. The school has showers for the gym." He pulled out an envelope with David's writing. It was all torn up and looked worn out. "I saw he put that in the mailing box, but I didn't know it had money in it. I figured it was for you, and you wouldn't want grandma to hold it for you, but it got wet along with my research papers, and well, I figured if he left it for you, I could use it too, as long as I was responsible."

"You're a smart young man," David remarked.

Charles narrowed his eyes warily. "You have no idea."

She squeezed her son in caution. They'd talked about how most adults didn't like knowing a child was more intelligent than them, especially from the way Ingrid treated Charles. "And Grandmother? What happened to her?"

Her son shrugged. "She was constantly complaining she was going to miss the bus to go play at the casino. I don't think she even noticed I ran away because when I came back to the house a week later, I decided to come home and get some more clothes, but she had cleaned out the house and the locks were changed. That was only two weeks after I left. I didn't know what else to do. I didn't want anyone to know I was all by myself, so I just stayed where I was at the school unless I went out to get something to eat off-campus. I had my scooter with me, so at least I could get around." He hugged her again. "I was in the campus hall when the news came on, and I heard your voice. Momma, don't leave me like that again, please."

"I won't, my love." She could feel all the stress leaving his body. This hug was full of so much gratitude, and she returned the hug with great force. She had been stressed, too, and knowing her son was alive and healthy meant everything to her.

"Are you hungry now?" she asked.

"Famished!" he exclaimed.

David heard them and quickly went to fix a plate for Charles while Gabrielle helped her son off with his coat and overly large backpack.

Dragging her fingers through his thick curly afro, Charles said, reading her concerned thoughts, "I know, I need to get it cut."

With his thick hair and his dark skin, Gabrielle hoped David didn't dare put anything together looking at Charles.

As usual, Charles pulled his mother's chair out to help her sit down before he situated himself. When David sat across from Charles, the young man still looked warily at him.

David introduced himself, "I'm David."

"I know," Charles said. "You're the brother to my mom's friend. She told me. You like to go around and leave thousands of dollars in strange women's mailboxes?"

"No," David responded. "Your mother deserved that money to help herself."

"We're fine now." Charles took the money out of his pocket and pushed it across the table to David. "I can pay you back this summer when I get a job."

"No payback is necessary." David pushed the money to Gabrielle. "You're pretty young to be working."

Charles leaned forward. "You're pretty desperate to be chasing after your deceased brother's friend."

Gabrielle put her hand on Charles to calm her son's snippiness. "David helped me. He's been helping me."

"He's your friend now?" Charles asked.

After David admitted he loved her, she felt the man was more than a friend. "You should be thanking him, Charles. David helped me get on the news and has been by my side throughout this ordeal."

Stiffly, Charles said, "Thank you, Mr. David."

Gabrielle was glad her son was still respectful, but she knew Charles would be the smarty pants, no matter what.

"There's a room all ready for you here, Charles," she said.

"We're staying here?" Charles asked.

"Yes."

Her son looked back at the windowsill to see the flowers had been removed. "Just making sure it's for a long time." He voraciously ate his food, and she could see her son had not eaten a good meal in a long time.

When he'd practically licked the plate clean, he reached over and touched his mother's hand tenderly, rubbing over the area where she had the IV in her arm. "I'm sorry you lost the baby," he said remorsefully. "I wanted a sister. Are you okay?"

"Yes, Charles. I'm better. I've been ordered to get some rest for the next couple of weeks before I return to work, and I plan to because I want to spend as much time with you as I can."

"Tomorrow morning, I can take you to retrieve the items you hid," David offered.

Charles pursed his lips together because he wanted to refuse but only nodded in thanks. "So, Mr. David," her son said as casually as possible. "What's wrong with you?"

CHAPTER 23

YOU'RE LIFE IS MY LIFE.

David looked over at Gabrielle, who looked as confused as him from her son's question.

"What do you mean, Charles?" Gabrielle asked with precaution.

"Well, clearly, the slight yellowing of his eyes is a lack of deficiency in the body," Charles pointed out.

"Your observation skills are amazing," David pointed out. "If you must know, I have a condition that weakens my liver."

This intrigued her son. "You need a new liver?"

David answered, "Yes, but I'm not high on the donor list. There are millions of people before me. I don't have a common blood type, so I do whatever I can to sustain."

Charles seemed to relax. "I appreciate your honesty, Mr. David." He looked at his mother. "May I be excused to get ready for bed?"

"Yes, Charles," Gabrielle granted him.

Her son turned to David and said, "Thank you for the offer, Mr. David. I will see you in the morning when you're picking me up." That was a clear indication to say her son didn't want David in the house tonight.

"Eight a.m.?" David asked.

Charles nodded, kissed his mother on the cheek, and left the room.

"I'm-"

David held up his hand to stop her apology. "He's protective of you. It's understandable. He sees how people manipulate you, and he's just making sure I'm not one of them. I would be the same for my mother. His father is another ethnicity?"

Nervously, Gabrielle said, "Yes, he is, but he's never been involved in Charles upbringing."

David didn't press anymore and said, He's a very bright and respectable young man, I must say. You've done an amazing job with him as a single mother."

Relaxing, she said, "Thank you so much, David."

He looked down at the money. "I'm serious about you keeping the money. You still have to move in completely and make this place your own, and then there's the car and its expenses as well. The family lawyer should be contacting you by the end of the month. He'll complete the transfer of all the property and car over to your name and then anything else once it's all figured out."

"And us?" she asked bravely.

"And we'll take 'us' one day at a time until we're all comfortable. I'm glad to see Charles is back in your life. Now you can focus on resting, and I'll stay out of your way."

Gabrielle got up from the table, went to the freezer, and took out four bags of the milk she had been pumping. Quickly putting them in the to-go bag from the food delivery, she handed them to David.

"Are you sure?" he asked.

"How else are we going to keep up appearances until, as you say, we're all comfortable?"

David stood up and pulled her in his arms with appreciation. "Thank you, Gabrielle. I care for you immensely. I appreciate you deeply."

His kisses took her breath away. Gabrielle cupped his face and pulled him down for deeper kisses. He intensified the embrace, molding her body against his.

They both heard the shower water stop, which meant at any time, her son could walk in on them.

David picked up the money and handed it to her. "Your life is mine to care for, and don't ever think I do things in obligation to Oliver," he said, insulted. "You aren't pregnant anymore by him, so I owe him nothing." He pressed a kiss on her forehead. "You have my heart, Gabrielle."

She suppressed the urge to reveal her genuine emotions. "Thank you for what you do, David." Looking at the bags she had given him still in his hands, she promised, "I'll see you tomorrow. I should have more for you."

When David was gone, she went over to Charles' backpack. After removing all the old clothes and taking them over to the washer, she returned to the bag to clean out the snacks and then moved down to the bottom. There was a thick envelope, but with Oliver's handwriting on top.

When had Charles gotten this envelope?

Her son decided to appear from his shower with just his boxers on and a towel around his neck. He immediately checked for David and smirked with content that the older man was gone. "Is this really where we get to live, Momma?"

"Yes, Charles. What's this?" Gabrielle asked, showing her son the envelope.

"You tell me," Charles said. "That box you left I took, and although it took me about a week, I figured out the code."

"What was it?"

"My birthday."

She would have never thought Charles would have figured that out.

"I saw your name on the envelope inside and decided not to open it. I figured whatever your friend left for you was just for your eyes only. Plus, Mr. David's money was keeping me, okay, and I wasn't desperate to find out."

She hugged her son while holding the envelope to her chest. "I guess I should be honest with you since I need you to understand some things." Leading her son around the couch, she urged him to sit by her.

Charles snuggled closed by and patiently waited.

Gabrielle braced herself as she decided to be honest with Charles. "Mr. Oliver, David's brother, was your father."

Her son looked up at her as if waiting for more. "That's it?"

"What do you mean, that's IT? That's a lot, Charles. Haven't you been at all curious about who your father was?"

Shrugging, her son said, "A little, but I figured you'd tell me when you felt comfortable; plus, they say children get most of their inherited intelligence from the maternal side." His sarcasm was hilarious, and she had to chuckle.

The laugh relaxed both of them.

Charles continued. "When I looked at Mr. David's eyes across the table and saw they were like mine, I started putting things together, along with him leaving the money in the mailbox, and I figured this Mr. Oliver had to be the donor sperm."

"It wasn't donated," she protested. "I did care for Oliver."

"I figured because you wouldn't spend so much time out there and then investigate his death." Charles laid in her lap.

As bright as her son was, Charles still was a ten-year-old, which everyone tended to forget except his mother. "Mr. David doesn't know you're his nephew, Charles," she said.

"So he doesn't know I could save his life either, right?"

"What do you mean?"

Charles yawned and laid his face away from hers, closing his eyes. "I have an uncommon blood type too, Mom. Most likely, I could donate a piece of my kidney and save his life."

"Why would you do that? What about school?"

"No school until the fall...." He was near sleep. "I'll be okay by then."

"Are you sure about this, Charles?"

"He helped my mother," his son said obviously.

Gabrielle rubbed his back and comforted in the knowledge her son was her everything.

"He's nice," Charles said. "Mr. David is nice to you."

"Yes, he is."

"And I think he wants to do right by you, Mom."

"He probably does."

Charles kissed her leg. "We should be nice to him; Give him a chance to be nice to you for a long time."

"We should," she agreed.

Letting her son think he was in charge of their family was an old habit because she knew for Charles to work out his feelings for something new, he had to talk them out.

"I love you, Charles," she said, feeling her son going to sleep.

"Love you too, Mom," he said sleepily after a yawn.

She sat there and continued to rub her son's back, loving that he was home. Albeit, she missed David, but she was grateful to know David had allowed her this time with her son.

Charles was right; she needed to allow David in their lives and most likely tell him the truth about her son.

CHAPTER 24

GIVE SOLACE

Near ten, Gabrielle put her son to bed and then adjourned for her shower after turning off all the lights in the front of the house, checking all the windows and door locks, and then making sure all the curtains were pulled closed.

The large windows had light cream-colored curtains and no blinds, and she made a mental note to buy darker ones soon. These front curtains were easy to see through, and since they were at a window where anyone outside could look into the house, she knew that wasn't a safe option for her and her son. As a woman living by herself for so long, she thought about safety all the time.

Gabrielle took the double breast pump case in her room and made a note to probably put a college refrigerator in there so she wouldn't have to come to the kitchen.

By midnight, she had four more bags of breast milk. After cleaning the breast pump in her bathroom, she went to the kitchen to put the bags in the freezer, not bothering to turn on the lights.

A rustling by the front windows caught her attention just as she opened the freezer. Since there were no lights on, she used memory to put the bags where the previous ones had been.

More rustling fully caught her attention, and she closed the freezer doors and looked in the living room.

Her heart almost shot out of her mouth as she saw a dark figure's face pressed on the window. It was dark in the house, so the perpetrator couldn't see her standing across the room looking at them. The way their movements were, she perceived they were most likely taking inventory.

Was this a neighborhood thief? Some crackheads that saw activity and assumed they could break in the house now? Or was this someone she should know?

She made another mental note to let David know in the morning.

Cars passing down the street startled the figure, and Gabrielle watched whoever it was run down the road and around the block.

Calling the police, she added special attention to her home for suspicious activity in the area. The officer let her know someone had called just yesterday about a figure hanging out near the corners with a dark jacket on, but that was about it.

Grabbing a dark blanket from the closet, she hung this over the front window curtain and hoped Charles understood the meaning of her madness.

When she returned to bed, she was very much shaken up.

A text message came over her phone.

'You up?' David asked.

She responded. "Yes, I am. Lying in bed."

'So am I, but honestly, I wish I was lying next to you.'

Blushing, she typed back, "I wish the same, David."

Pausing for a moment, she wondered if she should alert him about the figure. "I want to tell you something, but I don't want you to get upset."

Deciding not to hold this back, since she was keeping an even bigger secret, she gave him the details of what had happened.

Two seconds after she sent the text, her phone rang with David on the other line.

"I can get dressed-"

This time Gabrielle cut him off. "No, don't. It's Charles' first night at home, and I don't want to upset him. I have special attention for the house. Something spooked the person, and hopefully, that wards them off for now."

"I'll come earlier and look around to see if any locks on the outside have been jimmied or anything," David said cautiously.

"Don't you have a business to run?" she reminded him playfully.

He kept a serious tone. "I'll be up early," he said. "I had to drive up south. After I left you, I got a call from the criminal hospital. Mina verbally refused her feeding tube. Since I was the only heir, I had to come and sign my custodial rights over to the hospital."

"You don't sound like you wanted to give those rights to them."

"As I said, she is my sister. I don't know these people, but it was the only thing I could do since I'm not there to access the situation, and I'm not driving five hours back and forth to handle matters for her when she decides to be difficult because she's miserable. I worry because Mina has a way of manipulating people." He sounded distraught over the matter. "On top of that, I find out a male nurse has been sneaking in food that's not allowed. He was also carrying messages for her out to the world but wouldn't tell anyone what they were and who they were for. On the logs, someone came up two days ago. I looked at the camera, but I had never seen this person before."

"Are you worried about Mina's safety?"

"No, I'm worried about everything else. With Mina not being able to move or get out of there ever, would she still try to continue her plan to hurt you?"

Her jealousy had prevented her from thinking that far, and Gabrielle cursed herself internally for allowing herself to get caught up in her emotions.

"I can't have that. I can't have Mina hurting you anymore, Gabrielle."

"Now you're just too nice again, David," she teased. "Keep this up, and I'll end up falling in love with you."

He chuckled, easing into her teasing. "I'll be sure to remember that. Did the doctor contact you about your drop?"

"No, but I'm not worried."

"And you'll let me know if you get sick? Or there's something worse."

"Yes," she promised.

"Then try to get to sleep. I'll be there early in the morning."

Gabrielle disconnected the call and, surprisingly, was able to get to sleep.

Unfortunately, at four in the morning, she ran to the bathroom to throw up yet again.

Gabrielle was confused about her condition and prayed the doctor could figure out what was happening with her body.

For two hours, she stayed praying to the porcelain gods. This was worse than yesterday.

***

When she woke, a yellow tulip and note greeted Gabrielle. Her son's message said that Mr. David picked him up early to take him to breakfast and run errands.

Getting to the kitchen after another round in the bathroom, she made peppermint tea and then smiled at the dozen roses in the living room. There was a note enclosed in an envelope.

'You are loved. David.'

Holding the card to her chest, she smiled so hard her lips hurt, but then she was back in the bathroom again.

When she was able to feel better, she fixed herself some toast and then pumped some milk before laying down. The next time she woke, she could feel Charles kissing her cheek.

Concerned, he asked, "Are you okay?"

"Yes," she said, but it was a lie. She felt exhausted, but she was starting to get hungry since it was in the afternoon. "Thank you for the flower."

"Mr. David brought it when he brought the other ones. He told me to leave it on your pillow with a note. I like him, Mom. He thinks of things to make you happy. He even brought some soup for you. I let him know your favorite kind," Charles said. "Mom, when are we going to tell him about me?"

"I don't know. I need more time. That's a huge thing, and I don't think I want him to know just yet."

"But he needs us as much as we need him," Charles pointed out.

Perhaps she didn't want David to be with her because she controlled his legacy, and she liked knowing he was there because he loved her! Or maybe she needed assurance to realize she loved him and not because he looked like Oliver.

Charles was right, David was wonderful to her, and she had started to love this man and think of Oliver less and less when she was with David. "Soon, Charles. I'll tell him soon."

"Like in a day, soon? Or like longer?" her son pressed.

"Sooner than longer," she promised.

"Are you going to eat your soup? Mr. David is waiting in the living room to say hello."

She knew Charles wasn't going to leave until she got out of bed, so she pushed herself up and got up. "Let me use the bathroom, and I'll be in there with you too."

"I'm going to be in my room. I want to put up all my things and make sure my experiments don't get messed up. Mr. David bought me some shelves and tables for my room. Oh, and he also bought me a phone! I have a lot to set up. Is that okay?"

"It's always okay," she said and kissed her son.

Charles left, and she noticed she had a couple of missed calls. They were from the doctor's office, and she cursed herself for forgetting her doctor's appointment by oversleeping.

A link to reschedule had been emailed to her, as the voice message from the doctor's office said. Chance seemed pretty upset she wasn't coming in from his tone of voice. "I need to speak with you, Gabrielle."

After she rescheduled for tomorrow morning, Gabrielle cleaned herself up before joining David in the front room.

Upon seeing her, David immediately pulled her in his arms and kissed her as if he hadn't laid eyes on her since eternity.

She was falling in love with him despite the fact she was trying not to. The feel of his arms around her body warmed her soul and made everything better. She knew she needed David in her life because he was already in her heart.

"You missed me?" Gabrielle asked, surprised.

"Very much," he admitted and started to pull away, but she held him close.

"I missed you too," she said.

"But Charles could come out-"

Gabrielle interrupted him. "He's not. He went into his room, and I'll be surprised if I don't see him until very later on when he smells dinner." She was touched that David wanted to be respectful to her son.

"Good, because I need to speak to you in private," David said in a solemn tone. He handed her a card. "I'll text you the phone number to Charles' new phone, and I got him a lot of things for his room if you don't mind."

"Not at all, I'll repay you—"

"Not necessary," David said, cutting her off. "Let's get you some soup. It looks like you haven't eaten all day."

She curled on the couch while he unpackaged her food, and he talked.

"Mina is still scheming. Getting me to sign over custody was all an attempt to control the company again. I stopped in the office this morning to get served papers from another law office. When I released my custody over her to the hospital, it seems they assigned rights over to someone else immediately per her instructions."

"Why is that important?" Gabrielle asked between spoonful's of soup.

"Since you no longer have any claim over Oliver's estate, Mina is next in line to have the rightful next of kin spot, even though she is a criminal. And as of this afternoon, Mina diverted funds away from the business for her personal use. I hired an inheritance lawyer, Tyler Black, to fight my father's will, but I don't think there's much I can do since my father made it ironclad. No one wanted to touch it, but they said Tyler is the best, and I'm going to have to spend the rest of my savings hiring him to protect my family's legacy. I'm an idiot for giving away custody."

Putting a hand on his arm, Gabrielle said, "You thought you were looking out for her welfare, David. You can't blame yourself for being honest and caring."

"And just like Oliver, I realize how damn deceitful she is too late. I'm just so sick and tired of lies."

Gabrielle could see the frustration all over his body and wanted to assure him things could be okay, but then that would mean she'd have to reveal Charles is Oliver's son. Keeping a secret could mean losing David. He'd hate her for keeping the information from him.

"Everything is going to work out," she assured him.

"I hope. I can't let Mina destroy our family with her greed anymore."

She knew David was very frustrated and decided to help take his mind off of things. Tugging on his hand, she guided him into her bedroom. David didn't hesitate and came with her. After locking the door, he let her help him off with his jacket and joined her on the bed. Opening the front of her nightgown gave him easy access to her nipples.

David didn't hesitate to latch on.

If she couldn't give him peace right now, she could provide him with solace. ☐

THE TROUBLE WITH GABRIELLE

Chapter 25

This Can't Be Happening Again

During dinner, Charles was a chatterbox exuberant about his experiments still being viable. She was used to his fast talk and enthusiasm, but David was becoming just as excited as her son.

David offered to help her with the dishes. Secretly, David would find ways to kiss her neck or touch her body, to keep her highly aroused. Gabrielle was eagerly trying to figure out how to keep David after dinner when Charles rushed into the kitchen, announcing they'd be watching his favorite movie in the living room.

David was all in agreement, but only because he'd never seen the Disney classic, while Gabrielle had seen this move over a hundred times. Charles knew the movie by heart, often reciting lines and songs loudly but laughing uproariously as if he'd never seen the movie before.

Somehow, Charles drifted to sleep near the movie's ending, and David carried him to his bed. Gabrielle listened and watched a little bit out of sight by the bedroom door.

"Mr. David," Sleepily Charles said as David pulled the covers up to his shoulders.

"Yes, Charles."

"Mom loves you too; she just doesn't know how to tell you."

"I know."

Charles chuckled. "You gotta hug her a whole bunch."

"I will," David promised.

Charles quietly started snoring seconds later. David turned the room's light off and joined her in the hallway after closing the door.

"You're perfect," she said, throwing her arms around his neck.

He held her close, taking full advantage of her body against his.

"Thank you," he said.

Taking his hand and leading him back to her bedroom, Gabrielle almost couldn't wait for her bedroom door to close before she was kissing him. By the time they reached the bed, their clothes were gone. Gabrielle loved how his manhood twitched excitedly in her grip, and she enjoyed the taste of his secretion. She took her time, pulling him down her throat while her hands touched him from his chest to his thighs. Her mouth couldn't make up its mind to engulf his staff, lave away on his orbs, or lick all around the corners. David worshipfully approved everything, trying to stay as quiet as possible but being driven to mind-boggling sexual arousal. She loved his response.

Oliver had always hidden his emotions even though she knew he very much enjoyed foreplay and sex with her.

"Damn, Gabrielle," he hissed in a strain drawing her back up to kiss her deeply.

His body was primed and ready to join with hers, but David took his time, slowly moving down her body with his hands and mouth, tasting, touching, and exciting every inch of her body. On the one hand, Gabrielle wanted to scream the ceiling down but then thought about her son's bedroom near the front of the house.

David took her to several pinnacles and then finally joined with hers. Moving up her body, he pressed himself firmly into her until he rocked her hips. She joined his sexual choreography holding him close as her soul meshed with his. David's mouth descended to her breasts, and they culminated as he suckled her warm milky essence down his throat.

The sensation was blissful, and Gabrielle was delightfully helpless in his arms, unsure how long they stayed connected or how long he drew sustenance.

Sometime after their lovemaking, Gabrielle again awoke in the middle of the night to throw up.

David, of course, had been riled by her movement since he had fallen asleep on her chest, and their legs still entwined. While she rinsed her mouth out, he returned from the kitchen with a cup of peppermint tea.

"Have you spoken with the doctor about the continued nausea since you're not pregnant anymore?" he asked.

"I was supposed to see him today," she answered, following him back into the bedroom. "I rescheduled my doctor's appointment for today."

He straightened the bed and then let her get in before he joined her.

"I can take you since I took off from the office to go see the lawyer later in the afternoon. Do you think it could be serious, Gabrielle?"

Laying in his arms was the perfect oxytocin she needed to calm herself. Of course, she had thought of every scenario in the book, but she couldn't pinpoint anything. "It could be the nursing," she voiced worriedly. "I did lactate early with Charles, but I bound my chest to stop the flow until he was born. I don't remember if it had anything to do with the continued morning sickness or if binding helped lessen the symptoms."

They both knew what binding meant, and although it would mean David would have to find another for his much-needed nutrients, she had begun to love being his source. She had even started to wonder how she could continue this long after he received his kidney and didn't need to nurse anymore. Was that erotically strange? She was in an unknown territory of kink she had never imagined.

Gabrielle changed the subject. "Are you worried; Mina will drain the business dry?"

"She can't touch the payroll money, so the business can sustain for at least a year before I worry about not being able to pay employees. I'd have to figure out a way to pay any creditors, location cost, and utilities in the next couple of months if I can't get back control."

"Why would she do something like this?" Gabrielle asked, feeling his frustration.

"She's greedy," David answered. "And she could care less about this business my family created. And most likely, she knows how much this means to me and wants to hurt me."

Remembering her son's words, Gabrielle knew she needed to tell David the truth soon. Not only could this save his life, but it would save his business.

David didn't say anything else, but his arms were holding her tight. His whole demeanor told her he loved the oxytocin he received from her just as much as she was enjoying his.

***

The morning at the house was uneventful. Charles had stayed up late with his experiments, but she cooked his breakfast and left it covered in the microwave. She kissed him goodbye and let him know she was going to do some errands.

"Call me for anything," she ordered.

Her son only nodded sleepily and said goodbye to David as well.

"Do you think he knew I spent the night?" David asked in the car.

"I don't know, but I think he's very comfortable with you there," Gabrielle answered.

The nurse at the doctor's office insisted Dr. Chance Jefferson wished to see Gabrielle alone in his office.

"It's fine. I can wait here in the lobby," David assured her. "I know he's not a fan of mine. He doesn't trust me, and he has every reason not to when you consider my stepsister was trying to kill you."

Chance entered his office a few minutes after she was seated.

"How was your morning?" Chance asked.

"Not well," she answered. "I'm still feeling nauseous—"

He finished her sentence, "Like you're still pregnant?"

Shifting uncomfortably, Gabrielle said, "I wasn't being sarcastic."

"I wasn't either." he opened her file. "I ran the test three times. You are pregnant, Gabrielle Payne."

Shaking her head in disbelief, she said, "I thought I lost the baby."

"You did. I was there myself when the remains were removed. Since this was a natural abortion, there wasn't a chance of us scraping the uterus, which usually is done after an unnatural abortion. A flush to clean out the area anything toxic, and you were closely monitored. It's a rare phenomenon called superfetation. I've dealt with other types of this phenomenon, which I was able to detect so fast. Any other doctor would have taken you through the gambit before realizing this was happening." Chance shook his head, looking in amazement as if she was the eighth wonder of the world.

Gabrielle's mind was about to explode at the revelation. "How could this have happened?"

"You naturally produce a high level of hCG, which usually dies down a couple of months after pregnancy to sustain the fertilized egg. The uterus is designed to stop releasing eggs during pregnancy, but in your case, another egg was released and attached to the uterus wall. You're four to six weeks, but since you were in the hospital during that time, I would say it must've happened right before the incident that made you lose the baby."

She knew... "David?" she whispered.

"The guy in the hospital with you?" Chance asked, reprimanding her like he was her brother. "Your former baby daddy's brother? Gabrielle?!"

"We... I mean, I was pregnant! I didn't think I'd get pregnant again, but he couldn't... he's sick!" She got up and began to pace frantically, biting her fingernails. "Is this because I nursed while I was pregnant?"

The doctor frowned. "You nursed another baby?" he questioned.

Gabrielle brushed all over. "I nursed someone," she answered evasively. "And will continued nursing hurt this baby?"

Chance assured her, "Oh no, nursing while pregnant won't hurt the baby. I think it's admirable that you're helping out another mother. Your body will adjust. When the baby is born, I would suggest only breastfeeding your baby the first week so it can receive the colostrum and immunities from you that it may need."

Her worry eased, and she asked, "Isn't it too soon for me to be pregnant?! How do you know this one is going to live?"

Chance came around the desk to block her pacing. "You're going to be fine, Gabrielle. Sperm is sperm, and your body was up and ready to ovulate again when you and David decided to procreate. Women are fascinating creatures. I believe they can take anything and make it stronger. You're healthy, and with proper rest, you could be holding your baby in less than nine months." He looked at the door as if David was standing on the other side. "I'm going to give you my opinion and let you know you shouldn't tell him about the baby just yet."

"Why? He's going through a lot. He needs to know. He hates dishonesty."

"Let's just wait," Chance said. "You're worried about the baby's health, and I'm worried about David's. Blame me. The stress of everything he's going through along with your health could jeopardize him and strain you more."

She had to keep ANOTHER secret from David?

Would he hate her more?

Nodding in acquiescence, she said, "I have to tell him soon, though."

"Let's just wait until this little one is another month, okay?"

That could align with Charles' "soon," but would David still love her when he knew the whole truth?

She held her stomach and closed her eyes. Would David believe he was going to be a father? Perhaps this was meant to be. David deserved something from the rejection and abandonment his family had done to him.

Chapter 26

You Should Have Died!

After leaving the doctor's office, David had gotten a text from one of his drivers. Some of Gabrielle's items had been found at a downtown pawnshop across the street from a moving company.

They agreed to go to the pawnshop because there was still time before David needed to be at the lawyer's office.

"You're strangely quiet," he said. "What did Chance say?"

"He wants to see me in a month for more tests,

"Is it serious?" David asked with a lot of concern.

She shrugged, hating his worry when she knew it would turn to anger because she had to keep the whole truth from him. "We won't know anything until I return," she answered evasively. "He said to blame him and said I needed to rest more, but he said the nursing wasn't harming me."

David blushed and held her hand. "You told him about us?"

"I told him I was nursing someone, but I didn't indicate whom, and he didn't press the subject."

"I'm sorry you had to go through that embarrassment."

"It was only embarrassing a little, David. I didn't want to give up giving you what you want, but I knew you were worried if I was being affected by it." She could see the worry lines dissipate on his brow. "I enjoy giving you what you need."

He pulled to a stoplight and leaned over, kissing her passionately. "Thank you, Gabrielle."

David continued to drive to the pawnshop, and when they pulled up to the building, Gabrielle frowned because she remembered this area. Often, Gabrielle would have to track her mother down on the streets to sign forms from school. Her mother loved to go to three bars around this area, "find" things, and then come to this pawnshop and sell them. Once or twice, when Gabrielle was about seven or eight, her mother made her go into the pawnshop to sell stuff Ingrid "found." That had been so long ago, Gabrielle had forgotten.

Glad to be with someone who cared about her, Gabrielle let David handle the guy behind the counter, and after a lot of negotiations and threats to call the police, the pawn ticket with Gabrielle's stuff was located.

A lot of her home items were still in the store. Gabrielle saw her furniture, trinkets, and even dishes were there. The pawnshop owner explained the movers across the street often brought over items people asked them to move to get money owed by the customer. The movers often split the profit with their customers, and this was no different. The woman who claimed to be the owner of the items was demanding more money, but the pawnshop owner stuck to his guns.

"Do you know her name?" David asked.

"Nah, I ain't never known her name," the pawnshop owner said, irritated. "But she is always greedy and rude as hell."

Digging in her wallet for a photo she remembered having of Ingrid with Charles, Gabrielle showed the man the picture.

"Yeah, that's the bitch," the pawnshop owner said. "She was ranting about how she needed the money cause she had places to go."

"Did she say anything else?" David insisted.

"Nah, but as soon as she got the money, she trotted right over there." The pawnshop pointed down the street to the large Greyhound bus station.

David checked his watch. "Let's see if we can find anything else."

"I don't want to make you late for your appointment," she said. "Maybe she took the money and went out of town for good. This junk held no value for me, David. Charles got the important papers and all his stuff. That's what was essential. Ingrid has always used me, and hopefully, now she never comes back."

They went to the law office in Downtown Detroit of Black & Knight. David insisted she come into the conference room to sit in the meeting with him.

"I want you to know what's going on," David emphasized.

Gabrielle sat uneasily but swore she wouldn't say a word.

Tyler Black was a handsome white man until he opened his mouth and snide remarks just fell out. "I'm not the nicest person, but I get the job done. Your case, Mr. Farnsworth, will be the most difficult and, I'm not going to lie, very expensive. Your father has an ironclad document, so you can't have any sayso over the business. Right now, you only serve in your capacity as an employee. A foreman. Unless you have a miracle in your back pocket, this might take a very long time, but I can't guarantee by the time it's over, your business could be run in the ground, and most of your family assets could be gone, including the house and all the properties."

Gabrielle bit her tongue and looked away.

"Did you say something, Ms. Payne?" Tyler questioned.

"I didn't say a thing," she said.

David's phone rang suddenly. "It's the office. Can I take this for a second, Mr. Black?"

"Oh yes. Go through those doors. That's my private office."

Of course, that meant leaving her alone with the lawyer and feeling Tyler's piercing eyes chilled her soul.

Gabrielle could barely keep eye contact as they sat all alone in the conference room together.

Tyler asked again, "Are you sure you don't have anything to say, Ms. Payne. Any thoughts you might have could help your boyfriend."

Instantly crimsoning, Gabrielle said, "He's not my boyfriend."

"I know two people fucking when I see it," Tyler said.

The lawyer's crudeness knew no bounds. "Do you use shock as a tactic to get what you want out of people?" she questioned.

"No, I use it to get the reaction. I need to know the truth, and it worked. I like knowing all my client's interests - business and personal."

Gabrielle knew this was a prime moment to have alone with the lawyer, and she'd be a fool not to take advantage. After looking at the door, David had gone out to assure it was firmly closed. She questioned, "Any children would unseat Mina's hold?"

"If you had not lost the baby, yes. As long as none came from David, any child with any Farnsworth's bloodline would usurp the step-sister."

"Any?" Gabrielle asked.

"That's what I said. What do you know?"

"Oliver was promiscuous. He could have other children."

"I've been looking into that. I started an hour ago into a birth certificate search."

Oliver's name was not on Charles' birth certificate, so no one would know unless she said something. "And then?"

"Afterwards, I'll start a financial search. Perhaps this woman didn't want Oliver to be involved, but he still sent her money, kind of like he sent you," he said, looking down at the file. "You are Gabrielle Payne, right?"

"Yes," she said, doing her best not to look nervous.

"And you had a relationship with him for how long?" Tyler inquired.

"Does it matter?" she asked flippantly and changed the subject back. "After the financial search proves no other woman, what then?"

"I can't predict my findings yet." He leaned over the table and smiled devilishly. "I'm very good and finding things, but searches like that will take a couple of days. You're right. Oliver could have something out there. You're smart, Ms. Payne. Any other ideas?"

"No, Mr. Tyler?"

David returned. "Is there anything else I can offer?"

"I should be able to give a summary of the new custodial in a day or so along with any other information I find out. The lawyer she's using is pretty shady, but I have my ways of getting the information I want," Tyler promised.

"I'll put an immediate freeze on the business and hold off any transfer or sale of properties injunctions by this afternoon. That should give me some time to find out anything or use her criminal proceedings to reverse business ownership over to someone else. I have to find someone else. Your mother's side has no one alive, and your father's brother died two years ago. There may be an illegitimate heir somewhere, but we could be putting the estate from bad to worse."

David left, looking worse as they got in the car together. Her mind was deep in thought as she wondered how well Tyler could search and find out the truth.

If he was as good as everyone said, she most likely should tell David the truth soon.

"I've got you worried about my problem more than me," David said guiltily, kissing her brow. "Let's get you back to your son."

Holding his hand, Gabrielle nodded as he drove home, still pondering when was a good time to tell David about Charles. En route, they stopped at a grocery store to pick up something for dinner and pack the house with snacks for Charles.

David parked in the rear next to her vehicle so they could enter through the kitchen. "I'll bring the bags in," David urged. "Check on Charles."

She opened the door and immediately felt something was wrong. The front door was wide open, and a chair in the front room was tipped over.

"Charles!" she called out but received no response.

As she came into the front room, her heart raced, seeing blood on the floor by the front door. Running outside, she came upon her mother trying to wrestle Charles into a vehicle, holding a three-inch, thick, serrated kitchen knife.

"Momma!" Charles called out frantically.

"Get your hands off, my son," Gabrielle screamed.

Ingrid yanked Charles to her chest and pointed the knife at his neck. "One more step, and I could give a fuck whose son he is. He'll be dead before you take the two steps to get over here, Gabby!"

Charles stopped fighting, understanding his life was in jeopardy.

Quickly, Gabrielle looked over Charles's body, but he wasn't bleeding, but there was blood pouring from Ingrid's legs, soaking her shoe. Whatever had been done, Charles had gotten a good lick in first.

"Haven't you taken enough from me?!" Gabrielle exclaimed. "Why are you doing this? He's your grandson."

"He's a meal ticket, you stupid bitch!" Ingrid snarled. "Just like you were until you became too old. And when I'm done with him, I'll toss him out just like I did you."

"How? He's mine."

"Not for long," Keeping the knife at Charles' neck, she reached in her pocket, pulling out a small vial of oil and tossing it at Gabrielle's feet. "You're going to drink that. The state will declare me his guardian because you're out the way, and I'll control everything."

A cold chill encompassed her. "What will you control?"

Charles gasped at the pressure of the knife.

"Don't play stupid anymore, Gabrielle. I was wondering how you got ahead. How were you able to stay ahead and put this smarty pants spoiled brat through a private school? And then I saw the paper: the accident and the murder. I had to know more about this friend. You dropped everything and went to go see." Ingrid cackled. "He had money. Lots of money, and you were gonna get it and leave me with nothing, weren't you?!"

Gabrielle didn't answer but looked at her son. "It's okay, Charles. It's going to be okay."

"Pick it up, or I'm going to make sure he never talks again!" Ingrid threatened.

"W-What is it?" Gabrielle demanded to know, picking up the vial.

"Same thing your lover died from. That greedy bitch told me how to make oil from the flowers."

"Mina?!"

"Yeah, I went up there to that criminal hospital to see her. Got a job changing beds there while you were passed out in a hospital. She told me how you tried to steal everything from her and how you made her destroy everything, but I figured out the last piece of the puzzle on my own. Think I'm stupid? You're just like me, Gabrielle. You are using people to get ahead. You used that man, and you're using your son, and then you're going to use that brother. You're more like me than you think you are."

Those words cut deep in her soul, but Gabrielle knew it was far from the truth. "That's not true. It all just happened. Meeting Oliver, getting pregnant, and falling in love with David, it all just happened," Gabrielle admitted, inching just a little closer. "But it was all because you kicked me out, and I had nowhere to go! I had to find a way-"

"DRINK IT NOW!" Ingrid ordered. "Or kiss this bastard goodbye."

A small trail of blood started down Charles' neck from the tip of the knife, just as tears welled up and started to run down his cheek. "Momma, no," he begged.

"Shut up!" Ingrid snapped. "Your mother ain't worth it, no way. She never was. After her daddy left, she always drove any man I wanted away. And she drove your daddy away. I'm doing you a fucking favor, little boy. HURRY IT UP, GABBY."

Gabrielle opened the vial inching arm's length to Charles.

In her peripheral, Gabrielle caught a glimpse of David coming around Ingrid's minivan.

Holding the vial up, she said, "I didn't ask to be born, Ingrid. Why are you punishing me like this?"

"I didn't ask to be pregnant!" Ingrid sneered. "I tried to abort you! BUT YOU WOULDN'T DIE!"

It hurt to know this from her mother, but Gabrielle now understood how she was raised and treated all her life. Knowing she was just a meal ticket clarified why she tried to do everything herself, including raising her son.

And why she didn't want to give her secret out to anyone, even David.

"I'm sorry, Ingrid," she said. "I'm sorry I was such a burden in your life. I'm sorry you had to suffer raising me, and now you suffer hurting me. Charles doesn't deserve to pay for any of this, though. He's innocent."

"Momma, please!" Charles begged as Gabrielle pulled the vial closer to her face.

Watching David come right behind Ingrid, Gabrielle said in her loudest voice. "I'm going to do it, Ingrid. Just so one time in my life, I can make you happy!" Raising a toast in the air, she exclaimed. "To the worst mother in the entire world! Fuck you, Ingrid Payne!"

Gabrielle moved the vial close to her lips, turned her face slightly sideways, and pretended to drink. David used this distraction to jump on Ingrid, grabbing both her arms holding the knife away from Charles, giving her son enough time to drop out from danger.

Dropping the vial, Gabrielle pulled Charles behind her. At the same time, Ingrid screamed in frustration and twisted her arms around while kicking David abruptly in his groin to wrench away from him.

Ingrid slashed violently, cutting David on the side, and then jumping back and swinging around to slash Gabrielle.

Observing the knife, Gabrielle waited for her mother to miss by slashing at her, threw her weight against her mother, causing them both to go down, while she also caught Ingrid's arm with the knife and punched Ingrid in the face simultaneously. The force of gravity tripled the impact, and Gabrielle could feel the cartilage collapse under the power of her knuckles.

Blood splattered all over Gabrielle, but the relief of seeing Ingrid's conscience leave her body was what brought her immense pleasure.

The knife dropped from Ingrid's hands, and David kicked it away. As police cars began to show up seconds later, David fielded the officers while she ran to Charles' to comfort him. Down on the ground near her son was the vial of poison.

They both were looking at it and then looked at each other to make sure neither one had any remnants of the oil on them anywhere.

When their visual search was done, they collapsed in each other's arms, glad it was over.

Charles took out his phone and pressed stopped on a recording.

"How'd you think to record on your phone?" Gabrielle asked.

"Grandma showed up at the house banging on the door. When I knew it was her, I pressed record before letting her in, thinking I could find out where our stuff was. It was still recording this whole time." He bursts into tears. "I was trying to help, Momma. I'm sorry. I shouldn't have let her in."

She kissed her son's cheek. "It's fine, Charles. It's really okay. You didn't know what she planned."

THE TROUBLE WITH GABRIELLE

Chapter 27

He Knew All Along

Charles was fine staying at the police precinct while Gabrielle and David rode up in a private car with the prosecuting attorney and Mina's lawyer. They'd listen to Ingrid's confession, and David determined Mina had someone still inside helping her. The unidentified person he'd seen earlier on the camera had been Ingrid, but there was still someone else.

Gabrielle was exhausted. It had been a long day, but she wanted to be done with everything, and confronting Mina sooner than later would put so many matters to rest. David was constantly asking her if she was okay, and Gabrielle kept assuring him she was, but internally, her insides were doing Olympian flip-flops. She should have been more concerned and asked how David's health was. She could tell he needed nutrients and rest but trying to convince him to wait this out would have been impossible.

"Are you going to be okay?" she asked in returned quietly in the car so the lawyers couldn't hear them in the back seat.

He briefly looked hungrily down at her chest, closed his eyes as if to control himself, and nodded. "Don't worry about me. I've felt worse."

Gabrielle obeyed and stayed out of the room as the prosecuting lawyer, and Mina's lawyer went into the room.

"You think she'll admit to anything?" David questioned.

"Of course not," Gabrielle said, knowing this woman would not stop until revenge was done.

David reached over and took Gabrielle's hand. "You know I don't hate you for keeping Charles a secret from the family. I understand you didn't trust anyone, and you thought I might use you to get what I needed." Kissing her knuckles, David said, "Whether I get my company or not, I want to be with you, Gabrielle."

The fact that he didn't want to whisk her back to Tyler Black's office immediately spoke volumes of his love for just her. Charles was right; David's feelings were genuine.

Relaxing, Gabrielle admitted, "A-And I want to be with you, David."

His grey-brown eyes danced around. "After we leave from here, I have a surprise for you."

A nurse came to the door with Mina's food tray, but it was just a bag that would be attached to her stomach.

Gabrielle showed her hospital work badge. "I know how to hook up her bag to her feeding tube. I'd love to help you."

The nurse, looking very relieved, nodded and handed the tray to Gabrielle. "Thanks. I'll be back to check the line and gather the tray. Ms. Farnsworth's not very nice, so any time I don't have to be in the room with her is a minute I'll appreciate."

"No problem," Gabrielle said.

When the nurse walked away, David looked at Gabrielle curiously as she pulled the vial out of her pocket and put it on the tray. It was still partially empty, and that was the effect Gabrielle wanted to have on Mina.

A pale young man with dirty red hair about the late thirties looking pretty shabby for an orderly came up to them. "Are you related to Ms. Farnsworth?" he asked.

"Yes," David said. "I'm her brother. Has she been mean to you too?"

"No, umm-" Abruptly, the orderly walked away.

"She has to be stopped," Gabrielle said determinedly. "I can't let her hurt us anymore."

"Us?" David asked.

Blushing, Gabrielle said, "Yes, David, US. Our family."

Despite Ingrid's written testimony, they listened to the attorneys go back and forth while Mina denied every accusation against her.

"I'll go to the car and wait with Charles," David said nervously. "I think Mina will be even angrier and determined not to tell the truth if I'm in the room."

"You're probably, right. But please, stay right here. I want to tell you something important when all this is over," Gabrielle insisted.

He nodded. "Fine, I'll stay out here in the hallway and listen."

Gabrielle knew it was time David knew the truth about the baby. She'd been putting it off along with her telling him her feelings for him. After kissing him passionately, she entered the room, putting the tray down in front of Mina. Their eyes locked instantly locked, and Mina's fear immediately showed, while Gabrielle displayed complete determination.

Around the room, there were faux plants of all kinds. Most likely to brighten up Mina's day because of what she did, the woman could never be around natural plants ever again.

Mina looked skinnier. Without constant movement, her body most likely had atrophied, and getting fed only nutrients through her stomach didn't make it difficult for her body to keep any fat storage.

The woman looked envious at Gabrielle's fullness.

"Good morning, Mina. Your attempt to kill me has failed."

Mina's eyes went so wide one would have thought her eyeballs were about to fall out. Her eyes lowered to the tray, and she saw the vial.

"Dinner is served," Gabrielle said, picking up the bag of food she knew how to attach to Mina's stomach tube.

"Stop!" Mina screamed.

"Why?" Gabrielle questioned as she proceeded to open the tube. "It's just dinner, right?"

Mina screamed, "NOOOoo! Don't put that on me!"

"Tell me a good reason why Mina? Tell us all how you met Ingrid."

Mina looked frantically at her lawyer, but the man seemed clueless about what was going on.

"She came to me. Told me she was your mother. Said she saw what happened in the newspaper. Said she needed to see me and understand why her daughter came up there to our house. I told her everything I knew - even about the baby. And then she told me about your son. The one you've been hiding from everyone."

"And?" Gabrielle demanded. "What else did you tell her to do to me?"

Mina pursed her dry lips together and looked away as if she had nothing more to say.

"Fine. If you don't want to admit what you did, then I guess it doesn't matter." Gabrielle said when Mina didn't speak for a long moment as she proceeded to put the tube on the end of the bag.

"It's poison! I told Ingrid how to make the poison that I killed Oliver with!" Mina cried out. "I told her to use my lawyer to get custody of that bastard after she killed you! We'd use him to make sure David lost control of the family's business, and I'd sink that business in the ground to spite him."

The prosecuting attorney looked in disbelief but glared at Mina's lawyer, who only nodded in guilt.

"What else?!"

Again, Mina pinched her lips together in defiance.

Hitting her fist on the tray, Gabrielle said, "When this is all over, if it's the last thing I do, you're never going to see the light of day again, Mina. You're never going to see another plant - even a fake one." Leaning into whisper, Gabrielle hissed, "And you'll never be able to see David or hurt him again, especially after I give birth to his child soon."

Mina's eyes narrowed, and she looked at Gabrielle from head to toe. "You're pregnant again."

This wasn't a question. Mina could tell.

Tears filled Mina's eyes, and she sobbed ashamed, "I hired someone to kill David."

A cold chill swept over Gabrielle, and she turned to the door. David could be seen staring into the window, and then the orderly came behind him. The young man must've said something to make David turn around, and then a loud boom sounded.

Running out of the room, Gabrielle caught David as he slid down to the ground holding his side while the orderly ran away.

Blood seemed to flow everywhere, and Gabrielle screamed hysterically for help as she held her hands over David's, trying to clot the wound. "David, don't die. I love you."

He opened his eyes and looked up at her. A faint smile graced those beautiful lips, and he whispered, "I know."

"And I'm pregnant with your baby," she said.

His look of disbelief filled his whole face.

She continued to explain, "I don't know how it happened, but Dr. Jefferson says I'm pregnant, and I know it's yours."

Faintly, David said, "Thank you," before he passed out.

Nurses and doctors came to help, dragging her away. Gabrielle screamed his name repeatedly, but David never opened his eyes.

From inside of the room, Gabrielle could hear Mina laughing hysterically in triumph.

"Now you know how it feels to lose someone!" Mina shrieked hysterically.

Standing up and glaring in the room as the doctors took care of David, every fiber in Gabrielle's body wanted to go in there and choke the life out of that woman. Instead, she closed the door to Mina's room.

If it were the last thing she did, Gabrielle would make sure David lived to make this heifer miserable.

THE TROUBLE WITH GABRIELLE

Chapter 28

She's gone

Surprisingly, Gabrielle was there when David opened his beautiful grey-tannish eyes again.

"Now I know how you felt after seeing me after so long," she said softly.

He tried to move, but she placed a hand on his chest. "You can't move, David. It's still too early."

"Why does my whole body hurt?" he complained. "He shot me in my side."

"He punctured a lung. You almost died."

"That still doesn't account for the other side feeling like shit," he growled.

"Well, that would be the new liver," she said obviously and then kissed him.

He looked confused, looking down at his body but also groaning at the pain of moving around. "What are you talking about, Gabrielle?"

"You're going to tear your stitches and wake up Charles," she reprimanded, nodding across the room.

David looked over to see her son sleeping soundly.

Gabrielle knew any prattling wouldn't wake Charles. Once her son decided to sleep, he slept hard. With the drugs the doctors had also prescribed, Charles wasn't opening his eyes any time soon.

A look of panic went over David. "Did Mina send someone to hurt him too?"

"No," she assured him, cupping his face. Unshaven, he looked even more brutal and sexy. "He gave part of his kidney to you."

That look of horror now went to concern.

"He's fine," she continued. "He wanted to, David. He said he'd heal faster now than if he waited to get older. And you'd have a nice ripe kidney, almost new."

"But he's just a child."

"He's Oliver's child. He was a perfect match, and since you were already on the operating table, Charles felt now or never. If you waited, you could get weaker, and he thought it would be unfair that his sister would also have to grow up without a father."

David pulled her to him and kissed her. Since she was leaning already toward him, this was easy to do, and she knew she wasn't causing any stress to his injuries. "Marry me," he ordered.

Gabrielle felt breathless. "David, you're delirious from the drugs."

"I'm perfectly in my right mind," he said. "I know you love me, and I love you. I want to spend the rest of my life with you. I want to make a real family. One thing I never thought I could. You're the key to the future I want, and I don't ever want to lose you."

How long had she waited for any man to say that to her?

Tears welled in her eyes, and she hugged him - a little too tight because he winced. Pulling away apologetically, she explained, "I don't know my strength."

"How long have I been out?" David asked.

"About four days, but they said most of it was from exhaustion and a need for your body to heal," she answered. "I went to that lawyer and presented Charles' birth certificate, and all the DNA Tyler Black needed to prove Charles was Oliver's son. By the time you get out of the hospital, I can guarantee you can run your family business. You don't have to marry me, David. I would've given that to you."

"I want to be with you, Gabrielle. For the rest of my life. I've wanted to be with you from the moment I first set eyes on you, I just didn't know it, but the attraction was always there," he confessed. "I saw the specialness Oliver had seen as well. You are beautiful inside and out."

"It could be all the trouble I attract," she said bashfully.

"It's good trouble, and I want to be there for you through everything, Gabrielle. I never want you to face anything alone ever again. "

David pulled her more on the bed. "Gabrielle, are you going to marry me?"

She was still stunned at the idea despite everything she had done and said to dissuade him, David was still asking her for matrimony.

"Mom!" Charles exclaimed. "Say yes!"

"Charles?!" she cried. "How long have you been listening?"

"When he asked you the first time," her son threw a yawn as he carefully stretched. "I'm too sleepy to stay up any longer."

Looking back at David, she said, "Yes, David. I'll marry you."

"Finally," Charles said and turned his head away from them to go back to sleep.

David kissed her passionately.

The door to the hospital room opened, and Dr. Chance Jefferson entered, looking quite skeptically at them, while he closed the curtains around Charles' bed area.

"Are you still healing, Mr. Farnsworth?" The doctor checked the chart. "Any undue movement on your stitches could tear them."

"I'm fine," David snarled. "Don't you have work to do?"

"I was coming to check on my patient, Ms. Payne."

"I'm better," she said.

Chance cut his eyes at David before he asked Gabrielle, "Does he understand you'll need to be on bed rest very soon?"

David's hand tenderly moved over her stomach. "I'll do anything it takes to make sure she's well taken care of."

"And?" the doctor demanded.

"And I'll make sure we're married way before then. I should be back on my feet in a couple of months or so, with rehabilitation."

This answer seemed to relax the doctor. He took out a wrapped up newspaper from his coat and placed it on the bed. "I'm sorry for your loss, Gabrielle, but I will expect an invitation for the nuptials."

As she watched the doctor leave, she knew the latter sentence was an order, not a request.

"Will he always be around?" David asked, annoyed.

"As long as we continue to have babies," she said.

This brightened his mood. "In that case, I won't mind him... much."

Gabrielle chuckled while picking up the paper, but her mood suddenly saddened. In the bottom right-hand corner, she saw the face of the red-headed orderly. She read the article, stating, "Jerry Butcher was finally apprehended by the police but not before claiming one last victim. He confessed Mina Farnsworth paid him to kill her stepbrother, David Farnsworth, and Ingrid Payne. Ms. Farnsworth is already serving life in prison at the Federal Medical Center in Lexington, Kentucky. Since acquiring an assassin over state lines, Ms. Farnsworth was charged with federal felonious crimes with no chance of parole.

"Stop reading," David ordered, pulling the paper from her view so she could look at him. "I'm so sorry you had to go through everything."

"It's not your fault," Gabrielle teased. "She probably got upset because I'd only drink your tea."

David looked guilty. "Yeah, that's another thing; I should probably tell you something." He struggled to sit up despite the pain he was in. "I think you need to know; I've kept something from you."

She tried to speak, but he gently put a finger over her lips.

"I'm not as nice as I perceive to be, Gabrielle. Just like Oliver, I've had my selfish reasons for staying by you, and before you take my hand in marriage with me, I think I should be candid with you as you have done with me." He put a hand on her stomach, and she could tell he was fighting the fatigue.

He took a moment as he looked down at his hand and worshipfully treasured her pregnancy.

"You're beautiful. I know why Oliver fell for you. You've got this healing spirit about you, not only in your soul but also physically. I tried to deny the connection when I initially met you, but the attraction...." His voice lingered as his hand moved slowly down the side of her face, her neck, and then across her shirt, almost touching the top of her breasts. Immediately she could feel the swell in her chest. "I could almost smell your essence, Gabrielle."

She had to close her eyes for a moment as the memories of him feeding brought her close to orgasm. David was right; the attraction between them was quite powerful.

David softly continued, "I knew I needed you, and whether I tested you or not, I wanted to taste you." His hand moved down between her breasts and back to her stomach. "That's why I made your tea instead of letting Mina do it. I added peppermint to help ease the nauseousness, but the tea was Milkmaid tea, made to initiate let down and increase production."

The confession blew her mind.

Sliding off the bed, she started to pace as she realized what he had done from the beginning. "You intended to use me?"

"I knew it would happen eventually, but not as fast and not as much," he admitted.

"Because you didn't know I already let down early."

"That would explain the amount," he said.

"Your confession would explain a lot from your reaction. No man has ever reacted so... naturally."

"Gabrielle-"

She cut him off, holding her hand up. "Unless you have something else fucked up to tell me, David, just stop talking. You knew people had manipulated me. You knew I was sick and tired of being used, but all the while, you were telling me you understood you were doing the same?!"

"Yes!" he admitted firmly without hesitation.

Sadly, he was the first person in her life that had outright admitted the wrong he'd done to her. Leaning on the bed with her back to him, she cried because, despite all of the things she'd gone through, David had been a nice constant in her life.

Turning slightly to him, she said, "I should hate you."

His eyes moved down to her chest again but then back up to her face.

Gabrielle said, "You don't need me anymore, like that. That's what you're saying? Just like Oliver, once he knew I was pregnant, he just left. You're just man enough to let me know you're done with me, David?"

David answered, "Oliver was an ass, and albeit I'm his twin, he knew admitting his attraction and that you were pregnant with his child would do the same for him. My father was a racist, and he made it known to everyone when I told him I was marrying a black woman that he wanted no part of me in the family anymore. I still don't care how anyone feels, and I will do whatever my heart desires. I confessed because I wanted you to know despite the operation, I still crave you. Your essence, your body, and your heart."

Perhaps it was her turn to use him and not feel a bit of guilt.

Yet, David said, "I'll understand if you want never to see me again, Gabrielle, but I wanted you to know-"

She cut him off again. "Shut up, David."

Turning off the light over Charles' bed to make sure her son was sound asleep; she went to the hospital door.

"Gabrielle, don't leave," David said sorrowfully.

Instead of exiting, she locked the door and returned to David's bed on the side, where she knew she could lay down.

He watched her intently with those eyes taking her visually in, lingering at her breasts before returning to her face. She saw the tip of his tongue lick his lips and a hungry vibe move over his face.

Opening her shirt, she said, "I think it's high time I use you, David."

Crawling on the bed, Gabrielle sat up enough where her chest was directly in front of her face. David almost looked ready to pass out in arousal. As soon as she exposed a nipple, he hungrily attached and pulled her body even closer to him.

The relief of feeling her body being drained was just as intense as the high she gained, knowing she was giving her milky essence to him. His body relaxed, and soon he succumbed to the drugs the hospital had given him, but his mouth never stopped moving. His other hand rested on her stomach, possessively claiming the life growing inside of her. He switched to her other side, which allowed his head to rest on the pillow. Entwining her legs around him to hold on and keep him close and comfortable, Gabrielle used her arm to hold herself up and smiled pleasantly.

She didn't mind as he slept but still fed from her. She enjoyed allowing David to use her. Knowing after the baby was born, she could still luxuriate in the joy of giving David what he desired at any time he wanted.

Gabrielle stroked his hair, loving the feel of the black follicles through her fingers. "I love you, David Farnsworth."

He paused just enough to whisper back, "I love you, Gabrielle Payne, soon to be Farnsworth."

Giggling as they held each other closer, Gabrielle enjoyed how his mouth returned to feeding immediately as if this was the most natural action to do.

When he was physically better, they would marry. Charles would be their ring bearer, and of course, they'd invite the doctor.

Perhaps Gabrielle would continue to use the tea to continue her production to make sure she could supply her husband and the baby.

Kissing David's forehead, she snuggled in and used the control to turn down the light. In the morning, Gabrielle would finish the paperwork with the lawyer to make sure David ran the business without any problems because she would put David's name on the new birth certificate and start adoption papers for Charles to become David's son. It'd be his wedding present from her to David. She knew Charles would love this as well. She was very sure that the lawyer would help her out because it was in his client's best interest.

Gabrielle would not be manipulated ever again. She would not be alone anymore but loved; Loved by a man who wanted and needed her in all aspects of his life.

And she'd be happy... forever.

THE END
20210928 -57871

The Author thanks you for supporting her writing endeavor and invites you to write a review for this book at the place you purchased or in the comment section at
www.sylviahubbard.com/troublewithgabrielle

In the review answer these questions about the book:
- How realistic did you find the characters and the situation?
- Was this a Happily ever after to you?
- What did you feel about Gabrielle and her distrust of the family?
- Was David's deceit worse than his brothers when it came to using Gabrielle?
- Did Mina and Ingrid get justice for what they did?
- Overall, how did this storyline move you or make you feel?

Thank you in advance.
Your Author, Sylvia Hubbard

ABOUT THIS AUTHOR:

Detroit Author & Founder of Motown Writers Network, Sylvia Hubbard has published over 50 books on suspense romance.

As a happily divorced, but wonderfully remarried mother of three, Sylvia has received numerous awards and recognitions for her literary and community work such as the Spirit of Detroit from Detroit City Council and State of Michigan Governor's Certificate of Tribute Emerging Minority Business Leader Award. She's spoken all over the United States and Canada about independent publishing, social media, 21st Guide to Marketing for writers and authors, How Readers can make money promoting their favorite authors and even how to be a Mompreneur.

Recognized as an avid blogger by HoneyTech Blogs, Ms. Hubbard runs over five blogs including How To Love A Black Woman, is CEO of HubBooks, Founder of Motown Writers & the Michigan Literary Network and has had seven #1 Best Sellers on Amazon. She is also a speaker, story podcaster, literary encouragement doula & busy mompreneur expert.

Related Links:
http://MotownWriters.com
http://HowToEbook.org

This author thanks you for your support to her literary endeavors. There are more books to read especially the Heart Family and the Cytee Brothers. You can also check out Kimberly and Jaelen Gates story in the full-length standalone book called Stealing Innocence I. Check out and collect over forty stories for your reading pleasure. Visit her website now. http://sylviahubbard.com

Support this author, by downloading or purchasing more books from her, reviewing this book from place of purchase and/or then sharing this author on your social network to encourage your reading friends to purchase her work. Thank you in advance for your support.

Connect Online to Sylvia Hubbard:
Twitter: http://twitter.com/SylviaHubbard1
Youtube: http://youtube.com/SylviaHubbard1
Instagram: http://instagram.com/SylviaHubbard1
Facebook Reader Group:
http://facebook.com/groups/SylviaHubbardLitWorld
Website: http://SylviaHubbard.com
My blog: http://SylviaHubbard.com/blog

Want another book to read now?
http://sylviahubbard.com/books